# Christmas *at* Sabal Palms

# Terry Overton

## Christmas *at* Sabal Palms

*Sabal Palms*
A NOVELLA

## AMBASSADOR INTERNATIONAL
GREENVILLE, SOUTH CAROLINA & BELFAST, NORTHERN IRELAND

www.ambassador-international.com

# Christmas at Sabal Palms

ISBN: 978-1-64960-448-4
eISBN: 978-1-64960-497-2
Library of Congress Control Number: 2022946961s

Cover design by Hannah Linder Designs
Interior typesetting by Dentelle Design
Edited by Katie Cruice Smith

AMBASSADOR INTERNATIONAL
Emerald House
411 University Ridge, Suite B14
Greenville, SC 29601
United States
www.ambassador-international.com

AMBASSADOR BOOKS
The Mount
2 Woodstock Link
Belfast, BT6 8DD
Northern Ireland, United Kingdom
www.ambassadormedia.co.uk

The colophon is a trademark of Ambassador, a Christian publishing company.

# Chapter One

Elaine was cutting it close. She had only a few hours, and there was much left to do. Mary, Adriana, and Bonnie were set to come over that evening to begin the first of the Christmas festivities. The first thing she needed to do was to somehow get herself in the spirit to decorate her Christmas tree. She opened her front door, stepped out into the warm, humid air, and made another trip to the storage shed on the side of her beach cottage.

The rustling palm fronds in the sea breeze announced today would be another hot day in Sabal Palms. The first day of December was often as warm as any spring or early summer day. But today, the morning air felt unusually warm.

In the small storage room on the north side of her deck, she stretched her arm to the top shelf, reached the tattered cardboard box marked "Christmas," and pulled it down. She closed the storage shed door with her foot and looked down at her bewildered miniature schnauzer, Bella, who had followed her for ten previous trips to the storage room and back. Bella displayed her tiny, panting tongue, which moved relentlessly up and down. "Last box, girl—I promise."

Bella turned her head, wagged her nub of a tail, and toddled behind Elaine inside the beach cottage door.

"Every year I think we put our decorations up earlier, Miss Bella. What do you think?"

Bella wiggled her tail.

"No matter. It gets me in the Christmas spirit even in the warm weather, and that is always a good thing."

Elaine adjusted the wall thermostat two degrees lower, triggering a swishing sound of cooler air blasting through the living room. The temperature outside had already reached ninety degrees at ten a.m., and the unseasonable heatwave was forecast to continue through the week. It didn't seem like it was December, and cooler air indoors was required to encourage Elaine's own Christmas mood.

"I know what we need!" Elaine announced to Bella. "Christmas music!" Bella only stared with her small, dark eyes and watched Elaine shuffle through her CD collection until she found one of her favorites: classic Christmas carols.

"There. That's better! As soon as I can get a few twinkle lights shining around the kitchen and living room, it will seem like Christmas *is* about to arrive."

Elaine opened the first box from storage among several sitting in her living area. She carefully lifted the eighteen-inches-tall Santa, decked out in a yellow and white cotton Hawaiian shirt; straw beach hat; and sporty, blue sunglasses; and holding a striped surfboard tucked under his arm. "Look at this one, Bella."

Bella tilted her head and looked at Elaine. The pooch appeared to be bored and sauntered off to her bed next to the sofa.

"Guess all the trips outside for these stacks of boxes wore you out."

With each unpacked decoration, a flood of memories and questions streamed through her mind. *When did I get this one? Was it given to me? Did I buy it during the Christmas craft sale in Port Isabel? Was it from a Christmas when the kids were young and Ed was still alive?* So many memories of so many Christmases.

She opened a small box holding the ceramic choir figurines and laughed out loud, startling Bella, who lifted her head and ran to Elaine. "It's okay, pooch. Just thinking about the day I got these singers."

Mary had given Bonnie, Elaine, and Adriana a set of small choir singers in long, white robes, holding songbooks. Of course, Mary had purchased a set for herself. The beautiful set of tiny, ceramic singers had one of their names—Mary, Bonnie, Adriana, and Elaine—painted in gold on each of the red songbooks. The mouths of the singers were opened in a perfectly round circle and gave the impression they were belting out a note. She recalled the conversations of that day years ago when they had opened the present.

"Oh, Mary." Elaine laughed and shook her head. That was the first year the women had decided that every Christmas, they would do something different and new to celebrate the season. And Mary had come up with the idea for their first new adventure.

\*\*\*

Mary gifted the set of choir singers to each of the women in a box wrapped in shiny red paper, adorned with gold ribbons and a tiny gold bell.

After Bonnie opened hers, she said, "Why, Mary, these are lovely! And look—oh, our names are painted right there on the little songbook."

At once, Mary exclaimed, "What do you say, girls? Shall we?"

Adriana, overly excited as usual, shrugged her shoulders, raised her jewelry-adorned hands, and gasped. "Shall we what?"

"Go caroling together. It can be our first new activity to celebrate the season."

Bonnie's bellowing laughter could not be contained. Neither could her words. "Horsefeathers, Mary! Who are you talking to? Don't forget, I have heard you sing in church! If it can be called singing."

Elaine gave Bonnie a disapproving look. "Now, Bonnie—"

"Well, I never!" Adriana frowned and chimed in with a scolding look, her arms waving about as any true Sicilian's would.

Turning to Adriana, Bonnie protested the objections voiced by the others. "What? Did I say anything untruthful? Tell me you haven't heard her in church. For goodness' sake, she sounds like an injured cow!"

Elaine tried to signal to Bonnie that enough was enough. But Bonnie would not be stopped. "Or a sick whale, or a dying great blue heron, or a screaming seagull, or—"

Elaine interrupted the string of insults. "Bonnie, seriously?"

"Oh, for goodness' sake, Bonnie!" Adriana exclaimed. Looking at Mary, Adriana continued, "Mary, I think it would be fun!" Adriana turned to Bonnie. "And I've heard Mary sing in church, and she sounds just fine! We could sing all through my neighborhood! Everyone enjoys decorating their homes on my street, on the outside as well as inside, and people drive up and down the neighborhood admiring the lights. We can check out the lights and all the decorations as we walk along the blocks and sing."

Elaine knew that Adriana and Mary, who lived in well-established neighborhoods in town with large porches and yards, had more capability to decorate outdoors. Where Bonnie and Elaine lived, right on the beach, they had to be cautious about outdoor decorating. The constant sea breeze and salt air could quickly corrode most traditional outdoor Christmas decorations, not to mention the occasional seasonal gale-force winds.

"Anyway," Bonnie continued, "I'm not a fan of traipsing around streets of houses with so many outdoor lights arranged in such a mishmash that you can't even tell what the decorations are supposed to represent. For crying out loud! Last year, someone put a giant light-up candy cane in the middle of a manger scene! And it blasted out 'Here Comes Santa Clause'! What is that about?"

"I remember," Adriana acknowledged. "I think Mr. Ryker's teenage son helped him with his decorations."

"Figures," Bonnie said. "Kids these days. Have they forgotten why we celebrate Christmas? Good grief."

Mary huffed, looked down at her "Save the Whales" t-shirt, and muttered under her breath, "Bonnie! You sound like an old curmudgeon!"

Bonnie heard every mumbled syllable. "Are you saying I am old?" Bonnie retorted. "We are in the same age group, Missy!"

Elaine tried to calm down Bonnie from now insulting everyone in the room and put a positive spin on things. After all, Elaine viewed herself as the peacemaker in this crowd. "Bonnie, it was terrific that Mr. Ryker's son volunteered to help with the decorations."

Mary sat up and seemed to be gathering her thoughts once again. She attempted to move the group back to the topic at hand. "As I was saying, I think caroling would be a wonderful way to get us in the spirit and celebrate with others in town. After all, last week at dinner, we decided were all going to think of a new thing to do each Christmas, and I asked if I could come up with the first new thing. Caroling is what I thought we could do."

The silence of the group could not be mistaken. No one was thrilled about the idea. Elaine didn't want to see Mary hurt by a rejection of her first idea for this new tradition.

Mary continued her argument. "I can get the songs printed up for each of us, and we can put them in folders and—"

Elaine looked at the figurines and regretted doubting Mary. "Mary, it would take a great deal of practice for us to get ready, and I'm wondering if we have time. And aren't our schedules pretty full of Christmas activities?"

That was the end of the conversation on that day. But the next day, Mary brough each of the women a folder full of Christmas carols and, eventually, had her way. The four women toured several blocks in town, singing out of tune most of the way. And that was how the new tradition of doing something different, something challenging, and something new to spread the true meaning of Christmas each year began.

***

In addition to the "something new" challenge each season, every December, the women took turns having dinner parties and inviting people from Sabal Palms. They took turns each year hosting gift parties to exchange presents. They went to Christmas Eve Mass with Adriana, and she went with them to Christmas sunrise church on the shore. And each of the women had family visits, or they traveled to be with family at some point during the month of December.

Each year on December 1, the women met to select Christmas trees and help each other decorate the trees. The tree-decorating activities lasted four days, a day at each home, and included refreshments or a light dinner fare. Today would be the start of the celebrations. The women would all go to the Christmas tree lot that afternoon to select their individual trees.

Elaine glanced at Bella, who looked back with sleepy eyes. "Wonder what new ideas we will come up with this year."

Bella's eyes closed as Elaine said, "Not caroling, though. Not going to open up that subject again."

Yet thinking back to that year, Elaine laughed when she thought of how agonizing the foursome sounded during their first practice session. Thankfully, they had improved enough that others could recognize the tunes.

Taking the small angel out of the box with a jeweled gown and satin waistband, Elaine recalled the following year when Adriana had surprised the women with her new idea of a spa day to celebrate the Christmas season. She visualized how each of the women had reacted when they had opened their own small, decorated angels with the gift certificate to the spa attached.

\*\*\*

Mary studied the spa gift certificate. "Oh, Adriana, this is, well, a treat. I have never gone to a day spa before."

Aghast, Bonnie spurted, "What? A spa day? Don't get me wrong, Adriana. I like to look good and all, but putting my feet into a tub of water and letting someone put a flashy color on my toenails is just . . . kind of strange. I don't even like it when I paint my own toenails."

Once again acting as peacemaker, Elaine redirected the conversation. "Oh, Bonnie, I think it will be fun and relaxing."

"Yes," Adriana continued, "I have already booked appointments for us to go together on the same day. We will have facials, manicures, pedicures, massages—the works."

"Massage?" Bonnie shrieked.

Mary's face had displayed how alarmed she was at the idea of a massage. "Now, wait just a minute—"

"Girls, it will be an adventure," Elaine insisted.

The women went together and had a grand day. But Bonnie and Mary talked for months about how strange it was to have people "putting lotions and stuff all over you for the entire day."

\*\*\*

Elaine placed the delicate angel on the counter to be hung on the tree later, and she set the carolers on the end table by the sofa. The larger decorations were placed around the living room, kitchen, and office. The tiny, white twinkle lights were strategically positioned on top of the kitchen cabinets. She arranged another set of twinkle lights on top of her entertainment center in the living room. Elaine's favorite location for the last set of lights was around her large bay window in the living room. Not only did the lights frame her window, but they also provided perfect ambiance for an evening of decorating a tree. She set out the flameless Christmas candles and knew batteries must be placed in each one before the evening tree decorating session would begin.

The remaining boxes of ornaments for the tree were stacked next to the front window. The fresh evergreen tree would be placed in the center of the front window later that afternoon. After lunch, Elaine and the other women would select their trees and then, as usual, take turns gathering in each other's homes to decorate. It was a great way to start each year and provided four evenings of fun, food, and discussion for their plans for the entire month of December.

Glancing at the four choir figurines, she whispered to Bella, "I wonder what our new adventure will be this year?"

# Chapter Two

The buzz of her cellphone brought Elaine's mind back to the task of the day: going to the Christmas tree lot.

"Are you coming over to pick me up? Don't want to walk in this heat. I might end up smelling like a wild hog all the way into town," Bonnie said.

"Oh, sure, I'll pick you up. I'll head your way in five minutes."

"Thanks. See you in a minute."

Elaine straightened her Hawaiian beach shirt and slipped on her dressy flip flops. She searched her small jewelry box and found her plumeria earrings, then placed one tiny flower on each ear lobe. A quick comb of her hair and a swipe of lip gloss, and Elaine was ready.

The humid air rushed inside Elaine's cottage when she made her escape to her car. It was almost two o'clock, and she hoped the evergreen trees at the tree lot would not dry out from the heat before she and Bonnie could bring theirs home. The truckload of trees had arrived the night before, and the tree lot had opened that very morning.

Bonnie emerged from her door before Elaine honked the horn.

Opening Elaine's car, Bonnie deposited herself in the front seat in record time and slammed the door. "Who turned on the oven?"

Elaine laughed. "It *is* unusually warm for December. Supposed to continue the next several days."

"I heard the forecast. I've been blasting Christmas music all morning trying to convince myself it really is time to put up a tree. Had the air turned down to sixty-eight degrees."

"I did the same thing," Elaine noted.

Bonnie turned to Elaine and asked, "All set to decorate your tree this evening?"

"Yes. I've already got everything ready for dinner."

"Burgers on the deck?"

"Yes."

"I made deviled eggs. Want me to bring them over?"

"That would be great. I know Mary made a sugar-free pound cake for dessert. And Adriana is bringing a salad."

"I hope Mary is putting strawberry shortcake together."

Elaine smiled. "I think she is bringing the fixings."

Bonnie grinned. "Think we will beat our record we set last year?"

"Record?"

"Remember, we picked out two trees in five minutes." Bonnie laughed.

"Well, they were standing side by side and were both perfect. We didn't even need to turn each one around four or five times to figure out which side looked presentable."

"Good point. And there were no gaps between the limbs. Pretty remarkable."

Elaine shook her head and laughed. "Bonnie, remember years ago, we waited until the last minute to go to the tree lot and didn't like any of the remaining trees? And we each took home Charlie Brown trees."

Bonnie chuckled. "Oh, my goodness, yes. They weren't much more than a trunk with twigs sticking out of the sides. But they looked amazing after we put all the decorations on them."

Visualizing the image of the two scrawny trees, Elaine laughed so hard, she thought she wouldn't be able to say what she was thinking. She could not stop laughing.

"What?" Bonnie asked.

At last, Elaine calmed down enough to utter her thoughts between giggles. "That's because we had so many decorations on them." Her speech was interrupted by another giggle. "We couldn't even see the limbs of the trees! And the poor, dried-out limbs bent all the way down to the floor! I was afraid"—she laughed louder—"the limbs would snap off before Christmas morning!"

Now they were both laughing to the point of tears.

"They looked almost ridiculous! Like blobs of Christmas ornaments! There wasn't much shape to them after we loaded them down."

"Oh my," Elaine gasped. "Whew. I've got to gather myself!" She let out a small giggle. "Well, here we are. Let's see what tree options Ramon secured for Sabal Palms this year."

Bonnie stopped chuckling by the time Elaine put the car in park. "Our town is lucky Ramon has connections up North and can get a couple of truckloads brought over here."

Ramon greeted Elaine and Bonnie as soon as they closed the car doors. "Good afternoon, ladies. Good to see you."

"What do you have for us today, Ramon? You know the kind of tree I like," Bonnie replied.

"White pine," Ramon said and laughed.

"Don't tease," Bonnie retorted.

Elaine laughed and listened to the bantering Ramon did with Bonnie each year.

"Blue spruce." He laughed again.

"Seriously?" Bonnie grinned.

"Cedar?"

"Ramon!"

"I am kidding. I don't have any cedars at all here. But I do have your Fraser fir trees right over here. And we have some Balsam firs in this year, too."

"Thank you, Ramon," Bonnie said. "But I will stick to the Fraser."

Like ducks following their mother, Elaine and Bonnie followed Ramon in single file to the other end of the lot.

"Here you go. I put these two aside for you ladies. I remember the height you like. And these both have great color and are fresh."

"Oh, these are amazing!" Elaine said. "And they smell very fresh. Look how green."

"We did it," Bonnie said.

Elaine was puzzled. "What did we do? Did I miss something?"

"We beat the record. Not even sixty seconds to pick our trees."

Ramon smiled. "You'll take these?"

"Yes!" Bonnie responded.

Elaine agreed. "They are perfect."

"Now, let me wrap these and get them to your car. Elaine, same as last time? One in the trunk and one on top?"

"Yes, they should fit."

"Okay. Give me just a few minutes. Where are your other two sidekicks?"

"On the way, I'm sure," Bonnie replied.

Ramon took the trees and purposefully placed the rope around the trees to form a net over each one. He put one tree in the trunk of the car, tied the hatch down securely, and placed the other one on top of the car.

"He makes that look so easy," Elaine said.

"Like he knows what he is doing," Bonnie agreed.

Ramon tied the last knot to secure the tree on the top. "There you are."

"Hello, strangers," Mary's voiced boomed across the tree lot.

Mary and Adriana sprinted toward Elaine and Bonnie. Adriana, as usual, was overdressed and over-jeweled for the task of picking out a Christmas tree while Mary appeared in her "Save the Turtles" t-shirt and shorts. Both women sported large smiles full of excitement.

"Hello, you two," Bonnie said.

"Fancy meeting you here." Mary chuckled.

Adriana laughed a little too loud and waved her arms about with jingling bracelets. "See, Mary, we aren't *that* late." Adriana turned to Bonnie and Elaine. "I told her we would be in time to see you here, didn't I tell you, Mary?"

Mary nodded. "She did. And, as usual"—Mary rolled her eyes and nodded toward Adriana—"thanks to this one, we got a late start."

"We've picked out our trees, but it wasn't difficult. Ramon has some excellent ones this year," Bonnie said.

An unknown man's voice interrupted their conversation. "Excuse me, please, ladies." The man, dressed in a nearly threadbare t-shirt, jeans with holes, and beat-up shoes, walked between the women and toward Ramon as if he was driven to complete a mission. "Hey, Ramon."

Ramon nodded toward the man and said, "Chris." Turning to Elaine, Adriana, Bonnie, and Mary, he said, "These are some of our first customers of the day."

Chris nodded as Ramon introduced the women, then turned back directly to face Ramon in an attempt to speak privately with him. "Ramon, about that thing we talked about?" He brushed his unkempt, brown hair from his pleading, brown eyes and waited for an answer to his cryptic question.

"Oh, yes, the job? Sure. I think I can use you for about four hours, mostly in the afternoon. You know how to tie these trees up like this?"

Chris nodded. "Looks similar to some of the knots I do on the boat."

"Great. Let me show you where the different types of trees are located around the lot and tell you about each one. Let's start over here with the Balsam firs. Mary, you and Adriana might want to tag along to see what I have in the inventory."

Elaine turned to the other three women. "Bonnie and I will head back and get my tree up. Should be ready to start dinner in an hour or two. See you around five to decorate?"

"Sounds great," Mary said. "Oh, and Bonnie's tree-decorating tomorrow? Same decorating schedule as last year? Elaine, Bonnie, me, then Adriana?"

They all agreed.

Mary turned to Adriana. "You want another taller tree this year? Eight feet at least?" Adriana nodded. "Yes, I need at least eight feet for the high ceilings."

"Okay, let's catch up with Ramon and see what trees we can find. See you girls this evening."

Adriana and Mary followed Ramon to the other side of the tree lot.

"Elaine, Bonnie," Ramon called out. He turned to Mary and Adriana. "Just one second, ladies. I need to speak with Elaine and Bonnie. Chris, show Adriana and Mary the group of Blue spruce trees over there."

Ramon returned to Elaine and Bonnie and stood silently.

"Oh! For goodness' sakes! Sorry, Ramon. We need to pay you!" Bonnie said.

"Yes, we do." Elaine reached inside her car, grabbed her purse, retrieved the correct amount, and handed it to Ramon. "Say, Ramon, who is Chris? Don't remember seeing him around Sabal Palms."

"Oh, he doesn't live here; he lives on the island, and I'm just helping him out through a rough patch. His wife passed away a few months ago. Cancer. He's having a tough time keeping himself together. He works part-time as a captain on one of the tourist boats on the island."

"That's why I don't recognize him. He lives on the island. Sorry to hear about his wife."

"Yes, it's been hard on him. Been trying to get him to go to church with us. So far, no luck."

"Nice of you to offer him work during the Christmas season. It can be a tough time financially," Elaine added.

Ramon put the money for Elaine's tree in his pouch.

"And here is mine," Bonnie said, handing Ramon the required amount.

"Oh! I almost forgot! Wait here. I'll be right back." Ramon went into the small office of the tree lot and returned.

"Four dozen tamales. Maria made them yesterday."

A smile spread across Elaine's face. "Oh! Ramon! This is wonderful. She makes the best tamales! Please tell her thank you, and we will be sending word when we will have our Christmas party on the beach."

"I will tell her." He grinned. "You and Bonnie have the greatest beach Christmas parties of Sabal Palms!"

Elaine and Bonnie beamed with delight and simultaneously said, "Thank you.".

"You ladies have a great day, and I will see you soon."

From across the tree lot, Chris motioned for Ramon to come to the Balsam fir tree collection being examined by Adriana and Mary. "Ramon, they have a question."

Ramon joined Chris and walked with Adriana and Mary to a section of taller trees as Elaine and Bonnie got into the car.

"Well, what do you think about that?" Bonnie asked.

"What?"

Bonnie opened the car door. "That poor Chris fellow. Sad story. I didn't have such a tough time when Bill died. But, after all, he was older. It was his time, I suppose."

Elaine put the tamales in the back seat, closed the door, sat in the driver's seat, and started the car. "It has been many years ago for both of us, Bonnie, since we lost our husbands. But Chris's wife— she recently passed away, and I'm sure he is still grieving. He is very young to have lost his wife. I know it must be difficult so soon after her death and at his age," Elaine reasoned.

"I suppose. He is rather a young whippersnapper, not an old fuddy-duddy like us. He has plenty of time to find another wife if he wants. Awfully nice of Ramon to help him out."

"Yes. Ramon and Maria are such sweet people. Our community is lucky to have them."

Bonnie turned and looked in the back of the car at the foil-wrapped package on the back seat. "Those tamales! Whoa! That smell is . . . well . . . I might just eat one on the way home!"

"Bonnie, can you eat those? I mean, with your blood sugar issue?"

"Party-pooper! I can have a bite or two. Guess I will behave and save my bites for later."

"Atta girl!" Elaine said, turning the car into Bonnie's driveway. "Now, let's take your tree inside. And then, if you don't mind, you can ride with me back to my house to help me lug the tree up the steps and into the cottage."

"Of course. Sounds good."

Arriving at Bonnie's cottage, Elaine and Bonnie looked over the two trees. "Well," Bonnie said, "you want the top tree or one in the trunk?"

"They are about the same," Elaine noted. "You pick."

"Okay, might as well get that one off the top of your car first."

Once Bonnie's tree was safely inside the cottage, she and Elaine drove the short distance to Elaine's cottage and took the remaining tree inside.

"There we go," Bonnie huffed. "I'll walk back along the shore to my place. See you in a couple of hours."

"Okay. Thanks for the help."

Elaine closed her cottage door, put the tree in the tree stand, and situated the tree a little closer to the window. She stepped back, and her eyes fell upon the four choir singers and the tiny, delicate angel. She wondered what new adventure the women would come up with this year. She knew it would be the main topic of discussion as they decorated each other's trees in the next couple of days.

# Chapter Three

Elaine put the last of the dinner preparations in the refrigerator as Bella scampered to the front door, wagging her tail and barking at the same time.

"Who is it, girl? Come on, Bella. Let's open the door and see who is the first to arrive. Bonnie, I'll bet."

Elaine opened the door, and right in front of her, Bonnie stood motionless with a large platter of deviled eggs and tinsel draped across her arms, shoulders, and legs. "I feel like a Christmas tree bearing deviled eggs."

"Come in."

"I can't move. I think I'm stuck on the stair railing or something."

Elaine stepped forward and placed her hand on the unsteady egg platter. "Here, let me get the eggs. What's with the tinsel?"

Bonnie handed Elaine the wobbling platter of eggs and remained in place at the front door. "I found the tinsel in a box. Remember after Hurricane Jada when we went shopping to replace all my Christmas decorations that were blown away in the storm?"

"I do, Bonnie. And I was very thankful my storage shed was one of the few spots only slightly damaged after that storm and that most of my decorations were spared."

"Yes, you were fortunate. Anywho, remember we found that discount Christmas store in McAllen, and I loaded up on boxes of everything they had?"

"Yes."

"I had forgotten I had accidentally purchased double the amount of tinsel I needed for last Christmas." Bonnie continued talking from her position just outside the front door. "It was a two-for-one sale or something. But as I unpacked the boxes earlier today to get ready for tomorrow night, I discovered the extra tinsel and thought I would see which of you girls wanted it. Trouble is, I had taken it out of the box and couldn't get it to fit back in the undersized box the way it was packaged. I spent twenty minutes trying to squeeze it back inside. No luck. So, I put it across my arms and around my shoulders to bring it all over here. The further I walked, the more tangled up I got."

Elaine chuckled at the sight of Bonnie imitating a human Christmas tree. "I'm sure someone will want it."

Bonnie remained frozen in place "Well, are you gonna undecorate me? Not only did I get tangled up with this mess around my legs walking over here, but now, I also got hung up. I can't move. I am chained to your steps. And this tinsel is making me sweat buckets. I think I have a heat rash."

Elaine laughed, darted to the kitchen to put the plate of deviled eggs in the refrigerator, and then stepped out to loosen the tinsel from the post of the steps. She began the process of unwinding and untangling the yards of tinsel. It was wrapped all the way around Bonnie from her shoulders to her ankles.

Bonnie shimmied her shoulders and wiggled her legs as Elaine gently pulled the tinsel loose. It was tricky because some of the tinsel was wrapped around other strands two or three times.

"What in the world?" Mary yelled as she got out of her car. "Are you disguised as a Christmas tree? Or the tinsel monster who ruined Christmas?"

Adriana pulled up to the drive in her sports car and honked. "Hi, ladies! Let the decorating begin!" She waved and clanked her jewelry. "Wait. What? What's going on?"

While Elaine continued to undecorate her, Bonnie repeated the whole tinsel story for Adriana, who juggled a large cobb salad and several bottles of dressing, and Mary, who held a sugar-free pound cake, strawberries, and a bowl of whipped cream. Both waited on the steps going up to the deck.

"My heavens!" Adriana exclaimed at the conclusion of the tale.

Elaine took the final strand of tinsel off Bonnie's ankles. "There, that should do it," Elaine stated.

"Good, let me get inside out of this heat. I never knew tinsel would be so hot."

Mary laughed. "Well, Bonnie, most people don't wear it like an overcoat!"

"Oh, you! I didn't set out to wear it," she answered.

"It was kind of cute on you," Mary teased. "Good color for you."

"Seriously," Bonnie huffed.

Once inside the cottage, the women headed to the kitchen and helped Elaine with the last of the preparations.

"Want me to get out the mayo and trimmings?" Mary asked.

"Thanks. Shouldn't take too long to cook these burgers. In the meantime, you ladies can start with the tree if you like."

Before Elaine could get out the door to light the grill, Adriana spoke up. "Wait! Wait! Before you go outside, I must tell you girls what I heard in the coffee shop today!" And with that statement, Adriana flung her arms up, with bracelets jangling louder than normal, and plopped herself onto a chair in the kitchen.

"Spill it," Bonnie demanded.

Elaine continued getting things organized for dinner and pretended she couldn't hear whatever juicy gossip Adriana was about to spurt. If need be, she would distract the group once Adriana got going so the conversation wouldn't be thirty minutes of gossip.

Even though all eyes were turned to Adriana and she was certain she was the center of attention, she wanted confirmation before she began. "Are you ready?"

"Tell us already!" Mary insisted.

"Here it is. I heard Trent Fortune was seen going into Edna's real estate office this morning."

Bonnie rolled her eyes. "Oh goodness, Adriana. Seriously? Of course, he was going into a real estate office. He is an investor, for crying out loud," Bonnie refuted. "That's not newsworthy; it's business, I'm sure."

"Business or not, it doesn't matter to me," Mary calmly said. "If it is a business deal, we will hear about it soon enough."

"But what if it *isn't* a business deal?" Adriana pressed, wanting to get the others interested in potential small-town talk which or may not be true.

"You mean, like a house? A personal property?" Mary asked.

"Yes. You never know. He has been spending a lot of time here," Adriana said.

"Oh, fiddlesticks," Bonnie said. "What do you say, Elaine?"

"Honestly? I say it is none of our business, whatever the reason. If Trent wants anyone to know what he was doing in Edna's office, he will tell us."

"On the other hand"—Adriana raised her eyebrows up and down repeatedly—"Edna *is* about his age, and she *is* quite attractive."

Bonnie, totally flustered now, admonished, "Oh, good grief, Adriana!"

Elaine knew she needed to get this train headed on a different track. "Ladies, want to go ahead and get started with the decorating?"

"Sure thing," Adriana said. "Elaine, you don't mind how we place these ornaments?"

Elaine headed toward the door to light the grill. "Not at all. You always do a great job."

"Hey, Elaine," Bonnie yelled out the door, "want me to start up some Christmas music?"

"Yes, thanks." Elaine turned back, opened the door, and looked inside. "Bella, come out with me, girl."

Bella, totally confused by the chaos indoors, darted out the door and followed Elaine to the grill.

The verses of "Let It Snow" emanated from the den. Elaine laughed. "No snow here, Bella. The temperature must still be in the nineties."

Bella wagged her tail and took a seat on the deck while Elaine grilled hamburgers.

In a short time, Elaine returned inside with a platter of sizzling burgers. The women dove into the mayo, mustard, pickles, tomatoes, and lettuce, and built their individual burgers. Heaps of salad and at least two deviled eggs a piece accompanied the burgers. The unseasonable heat found the women indoors for dinner rather than on the deck. They sat around the kitchen table and enjoyed the bells, chimes, and vocals of resonating Christmas music.

"You know," Bonnie observed, "this is the only time we are quiet."

Mary mumbled, "It's because our mouths are stuffed full of delicious food."

"Speaking of delicious food, I think I will help myself to Mary's dessert!"

The women chatted and filled the kitchen with laughter while enjoying a choir singing Christmas carols in the den.

Clearing the last of the paper plates from the table, Mary asked, "I'm wondering what everyone thought of that Chris fellow at the Christmas tree lot today. Did anyone find out more about him? Seems like a hard worker but haven't seen him around before."

Adriana said, "Seemed like a nice fellow. Quiet. And there was something . . . I don't know . . . "

"Unkempt?" Bonnie said.

"No. Not that," Adriana said.

"Broke?" Bonnie continued.

"Broken is more like it. Sad, lost maybe," Elaine said.

"Sad?" Mary asked. "How did you get that? Just looked down on his luck to me."

"His eyes looked very sad," Elaine noted.

"Never noticed him in town before," Mary said.

Bonnie quipped, "Because he doesn't live in Sabal Palms."

"No?" Adriana asked.

"No. He lives on the island," Elaine said.

"Where did you hear that?" Adriana asked.

Bonnie blurted out, "Ramon told us today. He also said this Chris fellow recently lost his wife."

"Oh my, then he *is* sad," Mary noted.

"That's too bad. He is so young. I'm guessing early thirties maybe?" Adriana said.

"About right," Bonnie said.

"But he works here? In Sabal Palms?" Mary asked.

"Part-time, I believe," Elaine said.

"Okay, girls, enough dawdling," Bonnie asserted. "Let's finish getting these decorations up on Elaine's tree, or we will be here all night."

As if they had just received a command from a general, the women marched into the den. Each one opened a different box and got to work.

Mary took a choir singer from the counter and held up the one with the name *Elaine* painted on the song book. "Oh, look at this one."

"That was a fun evening," Adriana reminisced.

Bonnie chuckled. "I'm not sure your neighbors ever forgave us for traipsing around screaming like a bunch of wounded shorebirds."

"We sounded fine," Elaine affirmed. "We were fine."

"Are you sure? Seriously?" Bonnie rebuffed.

"It was fine," Adriana said, waving her arms about. "Not one single complaint."

"No, probably dozens," Bonnie quipped.

"Anyway," Mary continued, "it was the first Christmas we tried our new tradition—our new adventure. It was exciting!"

"Nerve-wracking, you mean," Bonnie huffed.

"Oh, Bonnie," Elaine rebuked. "I think Mary and Adriana are right. It was fun, exciting, and, well, a learning experience."

"Yeah," Bonnie continued, "We learned all right. We learned we couldn't sing."

They all cackled.

"Then, the next year, we went to the day spa—" Mary said.

Adriana began waving her arms about in excitement and jangling her bracelets. "Oh, girls, I loved that one! Oh! I think I might just take a spa day again this year!"

"Yes, and the following year, we went to McAllen and made Christmas mugs at the pottery place," Mary said.

"Oh yes, I still have my mug," Adriana added.

"Me, too," Mary said.

"Lost mine in Hurricane Jada," Elaine said.

"Well, I lost mine, too. But we discovered we were about as artistic as we are musical." Bonnie snickered.

"Now, back to the topic at hand," Mary directed. "Any ideas for a new Christmas adventure?"

As if paying Mary no mind at all, the women continued placing decorations on the tree. Mary was always the most excited about the new adventure tradition. It usually took a couple of encouraging statements to get the others on board.

At last, Elaine broke the silence. "Mary, I like doing something new every year. It is a fun tradition. Now, let's put our heads together and think of something. And this year, I think it is Bonnie's turn to come up with an idea."

Bonnie continued decorating as if she hadn't heard Elaine's suggestion. Moments passed. "Wait!"

All sets of eyes turned to Bonnie's excited face.

"I know! That guy, Chris—well, he works on a boat."

"Yes, and the point?" Mary replied.

"Let's go on a boat ride!" Bonnie said.

"Horsefeathers, Bonnie. We have all been on boat rides at one time or another," Mary asserted.

"Not just any boat ride. Let's go on a boat ride in the Christmas boat parade," Bonnie suggested. "Let's participate in the boat parade!"

The room fell completely silent, except for the last fading notes of the song, "Hark the Herald Angels Sing" coming from the CD player. Bonnie waited.

Adriana looked at Elaine. Mary looked at Adriana, then back at Elaine. Bonnie looked frantically back and forth at everyone.

Elaine spoke up. "Bonnie is right. We haven't been in the Christmas boat parade before. We've only watched it from the shore. We love watching each year. Imagine how fun it would be to ride a boat in the long line of decorated boats in the parade around the laguna. It *would* be a new adventure. Bonnie, since it is your idea, you want to run down the details and see if it is even possible?"

"*Is* it possible?" Mary asked. "I thought the participating boats are all privately-owned boats."

Bonnie replied, "I'll look into it and find out. Maybe this Chris person can help us find a contact person, or maybe he would take us on *his* boat."

"Won't do any harm to ask," Mary said.

Adriana threw her hands up in the air and said, "Oh, I don't know. Check it out, Bonnie, if you want. But, I mean, a boat ride? Ever since poor Antony died on a boat, I haven't been a fan, God rest his soul." Her typical crossing of her chest happened like clockwork just like every other time she uttered her deceased husband's name. "I can hardly make myself ride on the ferry for a straight shot to the island."

Bonnie turned to Adriana. "I will see how it works. It will be fine, Adriana. I don't think the parade route leaves the lagoon. You can see land all the way around."

Adriana smiled slightly.

"Now, on to the next item of business," Elaine said. "Let's talk about our plans for the next few weeks. Of all the Christmas events we do, I think the celebrations we do the best for the community are the town party and the beach party. The people in town like to attend both and always have a good time. We get terrific feedback each year. Let's start with those two."

Mary added, "It makes sense. After all, two of us live in town, and you two live out here on the shore, so we should repeat these events because they are so successful. We get to invite all our friends to the best of both worlds: coastal town and beach parties!"

Elaine nodded. "I agree! A chance to experience Christmas in Sabal Palms from town to shore! What dates should we pick for the beach party out here and the town party? And which one of you two wants to have the town party?"

"Wow! Town to shore! We should use that for our invitations and put both parties on each invite," Mary said.

Adriana exclaimed, "I love that! Town to shore. Yes, let's use that. We can get the invitations designed at the print shop. I will take care of that once we have the details ironed out. Now, who should have the town party?"

"I loved having the town party last year," Mary said. "I would happily have it again this year if you like."

The discussion about the invitations and parties continued as "It's the Most Wonderful Time of the Year" began to play and the tree became adorned with ornaments. At last, Elaine began to feel the magic of the Christmas spirit taking over as the women steadily increased the number of ornaments on the tree. When Elaine hung the drummer boy on a limb, she had a thought. *Maybe this year, I should write a Christmas story.* She decided at that moment, she would do it. She had never before written a story about Christmas. Maybe she would even write a children's story about Christmas. It could be her new adventure in writing. She would keep the idea to herself, like most of her writing projects, until she knew the story was good enough to put out for others to read.

"What do you think, Elaine?" Bonnie asked.

"Oh, Bonnie, I'm so sorry. I was thinking about something else. What did you say?"

"Do you think this snowman is too big for this branch?"

"No, it's fine there. I like it. Now, what about the town party this year?"

Adriana, whose parties were on the edge of formal affairs, usually employed caterers for such events and had people on hand to serve the food and clean up afterward. "Of course," Adriana said, gesturing with her hands, "I would be happy to have it, but Mary, your house looks so charming when it is decorated for Christmas. Those pillars on your porch wrapped in garlands and the wreaths

with the big red bows on your windows! And your fireplace going—
it is always so cozy."

Bonnie, fanning herself frantically, said, "Might skip the roaring
fire this year, Mary."

Mary laughed. "Thank you for the compliments, Adriana. If it's
okay with everyone, then I will hold the Christmas party in town this
year. And depending on weather, I may or may not light the fireplace."

All heads nodded in agreement.

"Thank you, Mary," Elaine said. "And Bonnie and I will have
the beach party—progressive like last year. Entrées at my place, an
assortment of desserts and coffees at Bonnie's? Does that work?"

All heads nodded.

"And this year, should we add Chris's name to the invitation list?"
Elaine asked.

"Great idea!" Adriana exclaimed.

"Should we aim for the third week of December, like last year?"
Mary asked.

"That sounds good," Bonnie said.

Adriana clapped her hands and said, "Now that we have decided
about our parties, let's get this tree finished. It is looking fabulous!
I'm getting excited about this Christmas! I'll bet it will be the best
one yet!"

# Chapter Four

Elaine sipped her coffee, slid her feet into her flip flops, then turned on her Christmas tree lights. She had slept late. She hadn't planned on writing until two in the morning, but her children's Christmas story seized her, and she had no choice but to keep on typing. When the characters took her down their own path, she couldn't stop. And at times, her characters wanted to stay up late talking. This meant she continued hours beyond what she had intended. But she made more progress on the story than she had imagined for one night.

She placed a bowl of Bella's food on the floor. "Here you go, Bella."

Bella ran to the bowl and crunched the food down quickly.

Elaine's phone buzzed. She picked up the phone from the counter.

"Running late?"

"Good morning, Bonnie."

"Still planning on a walk this morning?"

"Yes, let me change my shoes and we will be right over. Wouldn't want to miss our morning walk on the beach."

"You sure? If you aren't up to it, that's okay. I can walk by myself."

"Oh, no, I'll be there in a few minutes."

Elaine switched from flip flops to walking shoes and tied the laces. "Bella, let's go. We're late, little pooch."

Bella followed Elaine out the door and down the steps to the warm sand. She ran to the green patch behind the house and did her business while Elaine attempted to rub the sleep from her own eyes. Bella scampered back to Elaine. Without thinking, Elaine began a conversation with the dog. "You know Bella, the warm, early-morning breeze is one of the best ways to wake up and start the day. Let's go." She hastened her pace, and she and Bella made it to Bonnie's deck in just a few minutes.

Bonnie, waiting on her deck, greeted Elaine. "Hey! I was worried about you. Not like you to be late."

"I know. I'm sorry."

"You feeling okay? You're walking slower than a hermit crab stuck in mud."

"Oh, yes. I stayed up too late."

"Let me guess—writing?"

"You know me pretty well." Elaine laughed.

"Well, it *is* about the only thing you do," Bonnie teased.

Elaine ignored the statement and changed the subject. "Are you ready for the crew to decorate your tree tonight?"

"Yes, indeed. I stacked the boxes of ornaments by the tree and put all the other decorations out last night around my cottage. I had time to get the lights on the tree, so all we have left to do is hang the ornaments. And I put dinner in the crockpot first thing this morning so no worry with dinner. Elaine, you sure you're okay? Our pace seems slower than usual this morning."

"Not sure why but I am feeling a little sluggish. You know what? I feel like a visit to the coffee shop after we get back from our walk. I think I need one of those wonderful coffee drinks with the double shot of caffeine. You up for it?"

Laughing, Bonnie said, "Yes, you do look like you need a double shot of caffeine, and you know I am certainly not going to pass up that opportunity!"

"Perfect. I'll swing by around, say, 8:30?"

"I'll be ready."


The bell on the coffee shop door announced Elaine and Bonnie's entrance. Elaine inhaled the aroma. "Bonnie, why does coffee always smell better inside a coffee shop than it does at home?"

Alexa, the barista, smiled when she heard the bell. "Good morning, ladies."

"Good morning," Elaine said.

"That smell," Bonnie continued. "It's gotta be the fresh-roasted beans! The smell overwhelms in a good way." Bonnie stopped in her tracks and gestured to a table in the shop. "Look who's here."

Surprised, Elaine said, "Oh my goodness. I didn't know Billy was in town. I thought he was coming next week. Bonnie, would you please order for me? I want to go say hi to him."

"Does a pelican eat fish? Of course, I'll order for you. I'll bring ours over to the table. Latte with an extra shot?"

"Yes, thanks." Elaine approached Billy's table.

Billy was so focused on his task, he didn't notice when Elaine and Bonnie entered the coffee shop and didn't sense Elaine's presence at the table.

"Hi, Billy. Good morning. You look very focused on your task."

"Oh, hello, Elaine." He stood up immediately and hugged her. "I planned to call you later this morning. Just getting a late start today. I got distracted on these notes. Needed a little caffeine this morning."

"Me, too. Needed a second cup of coffee. How are you? Thought you weren't coming until next week."

"I thought that, too. But I finished the recording session early. Got the whole album recorded in just a few weeks! Drove down yesterday."

"That's wonderful news! You got away earlier than expected."

"Yes. And I wanted to spend Christmas in Sabal Palms this year."

"I am thrilled to hear that news. You'll enjoy your Christmas here. Sabal Palms has a full season of parties and events planned. The season's activities start in just a few days."

Billy smiled. "I would expect no less. Looking forward to attending every one of them. Last year, I didn't make it down here until New Year's Eve."

"And that New Year's Eve was one to remember! The largest display of fireworks on the island in history."

Billy nodded. "It was something."

"I'll get you the list with dates and times for the month of December. Wouldn't want you to miss anything."

"Thanks, Elaine."

Bonnie approached with two large coffee drinks in hand. "Hey, Billy!"

"Hi, Bonnie. Great to see you ladies this morning. Elaine was just filling me in on the parties coming up."

"Oh, Heavens to Betsy! What did we count, Elaine? Two or three per week? And five big events the week of Christmas."

"Yes, I think that's about the right number."

Billy laughed. "I don't know if I brought enough party clothes!"

Elaine sipped her coffee and looked at Billy. "No worries. It's all casual. Beach clothes or jeans will work. What are you working on here?"

Billy glanced at the paper and pencil. "Oh, this? It's a list of ideas for a new album."

Elaine laughed. "My goodness! You just finished one album this week and already onto another one? No wonder you are exhausted."

"Yes, but this one . . . well it's different. Of course, I will need your help, Elaine, with the lyrics. And I've already talked with the producers and the studio, and they said it is a go."

"How is it different? Not country songs?"

"No, it will have a country feel, but this time, I wanted to put together a Christmas album for next year. I thought spending Christmas here would get my creative juices going."

"It sounds like a terrific idea. I would love to write the lyrics for that one."

Hearing the jingle of the bell, Bonnie looked toward the coffee shop door and gestured. "Elaine, look. Isn't that the Chris fellow from the Christmas tree lot?"

"Yes. I believe it is. He—"

Before Elaine could finish her sentence, Bonnie bolted over to the front door and stood right in front of Chris.

Elaine shook her head and smiled at Billy. "Poor guy. He didn't make it to the counter to get his coffee."

Bonnie rushed forward, wasting no time. "Hey, Chris."

"Hello. Bonnie, is it?" Chris asked.

"Yes. Just wanted to say good morning. You headed to the tree lot?"

"Yes, ma'am. Your tree, okay? Any problems? I can let Ramon know if you need anything."

"No, the tree is perfect. Are you working on the boat later today?"

"Sure am. I'm working an earlier shift at the tree lot today because I need to be back on the island by three for a tourist cruise."

"I see. I wanted to ask about your boat."

He laughed. "Well, it's not really my boat. It's a tour boat owned by the company that owns the Fish Fry Restaurant."

"Okay. I see. That boat, then, the company boat."

Chris wobbled slightly, seeming to be slightly off balance, and caught himself on the counter. "What did you want to know?"

"Is it in the boat parade? You know, the Christmas boat parade?"

"Yes." He burped "Excuse me. Yes, ma'am."

"Are you okay?"

"Oh, yes, late night. A little too much . . . uh, yes, I'm okay."

Bonnie continued her questioning. "What I wanted to know is if people can buy tickets to go on the boat for the night of the boat parade?"

"I'm not sure how it works. This is my first Christmas working with the company. I can ask if you like."

"Thank you. We girls—well, there are four of us—we wanted to go on the boat parade this year. I'll keep asking around. And if you find out about it, can you let me know?"

"Okay, I can try to find out for you. Want to give me your number? Wait." Chris pulled his phone from his pocket, dropped it, then picked it up off the floor. "Sorry. Here, you can just put it on my phone." He handed his cell phone to Bonnie and turned to order his coffee.

Bonnie put her contact information in the phone and handed it back to Chris. "Thanks again, Chris."

"No problem."

Bonnie sauntered back to the table, a grin plastered across her face.

"How is Chris?" Elaine asked.

"He acted a little strange. He reminded me of . . . oh, what was that fella's name? The guy who kept getting arrested for being intoxicated in public?"

Elaine thought for a moment. "You mean Henry? The guy who broke up with his wife and then went on a year-long drinking binge?"

"Yeah, Henry. Chris acted like that."

Elaine furrowed her brows inquisitively. "Are you sure? He wasn't just tired or something?"

"No mistaking slightly slurred speech, wobbling, and dropping his phone."

Elaine shook her head. "Oh dear, I do hate to hear that."

Billy spoke up. "Sounds like a sad country song. Wonder why he is struggling?"

Elaine replied, "His wife died."

Billy sipped his coffee and looked at Elaine and Bonnie, "I know how tragic that can be."

Bonnie continued, "I think you were right, Elaine, He is lost. But he said he would let me know about the boat parade. He said it is his first Christmas working with the company, so he isn't sure about how to participate."

Billy took another sip of his coffee, then turned to Bonnie. "Boat parade?"

"Each year, people who own boats decorate them with Christmas lights, decked out Christmas trees, blow-up snowmen, and all sorts of things," Elaine explained.

Bonnie hijacked the conversation. "Yeah, they travel all around the harbor, through the boat channel, under the causeway, and back again. Some of the boats blast out Christmas songs; small bands aboard the boats play music; and people dance on the boat decks. It is quite an event."

Billy put his coffee cup on the table and turned to Elaine. "You are all wanting to go? Have you been before?"

"Well," Bonnie replied, "we usually watch from the shore, but this year, I thought we could find out if we can get on one of the boats."

"I see," he said. "Bonnie, didn't you say these boats play music during the parade?"

"Yes," she replied.

Elaine, puzzled, asked, "What are you thinking, Billy?"

"I'm wondering if I might be able to get a spot on the boat, you know, playing music. Maybe we can figure out a way for us to all be on a boat in the parade."

Elaine smiled. "That's a terrific idea!"

"You know, Elaine, if we put our heads together, maybe we could work up a couple of new Christmas songs, and I can try them out on the crowd. Let me know when we can get started on the new songs."

"I am open during the day all this week. Be happy to get with you about the new album."

Bonnie couldn't contain herself. "You play on the boat? That would be outstanding! When Chris calls me, want me to ask him about you playing?"

"When he calls, ask if his boat is one with music, and if so, ask who I need to contact about playing for the evening," Billy replied.

"Be happy to ask him."

Elaine stood up, coffee in hand, and pushed her chair back under the table. "We will let you get back to your work."

"Oh, no problem. Just jotting down ideas. Bonnie, please let me know if you hear from Chris."

"Will do," Bonnie said.

# Chapter Five

Elaine dropped Bonnie at her cottage and returned home. She had several hours to work on her children's Christmas book, but somehow, she felt she wanted to sit beside her newly decorated Christmas tree and listen to songs while she read her Bible. She turned the Christmas lights on and sat beside the tree.

*Some days,* she thought, *I just need to spend more time reading the Word rather than typing out words.* For some reason, today felt like one of those days. She wanted a few more minutes of peace, a few more minutes of quiet, a little longer in prayer. Maybe she needed extra quiet time before she could switch from writing her Christmas book to writing song lyrics.

"Where do I begin, Bella?"

Bella turned her head and slowly crept back to her bed beside the sofa.

"Not much help." Elaine laughed.

She placed her Bible on her lap, and it fell right open to Luke. "Oh, my favorite place to read the true Christmas story."

As she read the verses about the message to Mary, Mary's visit to Elizabeth, the census demanded by Rome, the hard journey taken by Mary and Joseph, the glorious birth, and the shepherds in the field, she realized exactly the important things to touch on in writing

Christmas songs for Billy. She knew she wanted to convey the very humble circumstances of the birth of Jesus and contrast that with the glory of the birth and the glory of our gift from God: His only Son. She would focus one song on that. Perhaps another song would be focused on the promises made, even in the Old Testament, for the coming Messiah. God always keeps His promises. Then, she could write another song on Advent and anticipating the Christmas season and include the journey to Bethlehem. Then she would write—

A knock on her cottage door interrupted her Scripture reading and planning of Christmas songs. Bella leapt from her short nap and ran to the door before Elaine could open it.

"Wait just a minute, Bella. Let me open the door. Step back a little bit." She was surprised to see Trent Fortune, the newest investor in the Sabal Palms community, standing on her deck.

"Hello, Trent. How are you doing?"

"Hi, Elaine. Sorry to bother you. I was checking on some of the property out your way for the protective wildlife fencing and thought I'd stop by."

"Do come in, Trent. How is that wildlife protection project going?"

"It is going very well, thank you. The new investors for the community have stepped up and donated more money than I anticipated." Trent walked to the Christmas tree. "Oh! Look at that! Your tree is beautiful. But why should I be surprised?"

"Thank you."

Trent patted Bella, then walked toward the sofa. "Elaine, I am here for a reason other than checking on the project. I have been wanting to tell you something."

"Please take a seat."

"Thank you. It's just that, well, Sabal Palms feels like home to me. You know, after the accident last year and you helping me return to my lost faith, I visited my parents for the first time in many years. I made amends with my father."

"I remember."

"I have been keeping this quiet—or trying to keep it quiet—for the last couple of weeks. But I wanted to let you know. I am buying a house here."

"Here? On the island?"

"No, not on the island. Elaine, I decided to make Sabal Palms my home. I spend more time here than in my old place in Florida. I have more business interests here than any other place and thought it just makes sense. I am wondering, would you mind going with me to see the house? I would like to put a contract on it this afternoon. I need to decide for certain if I want this one. I respect your opinion."

"I would be delighted to go see it. When do you want to go?"

"I know it's sudden—and if you can't, that's okay—but could we go in a few minutes? If you're not too busy. I told the realtor I would call her back. She can meet us there."

Elaine felt her face emerge into a smile. "Oh, of course! This *is* exciting! It will just take me a minute to freshen up."

"Thank you so much. If everything works out, I would like to fly my parents out here to see the house for the holidays. If this is the right house for me, I can take possession of the house in a few days. And maybe someday, I can convince my parents to move here or at least stay here several months of the year."

"That sounds wonderful, Trent."

Elaine excused herself and went to freshen up a bit. She said a quick prayer for God to guide Trent. She already knew He would. He had guided Trent to return to Him by way of a plane crash. She knew God had this one worked out.

Elaine returned and heard Trent on his phone with the realtor. "Thank you. Yes, we are leaving now to go to the house. See you in a few minutes."

He looked at Elaine's tree. "That is one of the reasons I'm here."

"Oh?"

"If this house is a go, I want to get it ready for the holidays, and I won't have much time. I haven't had much experience decorating trees; and, well, to tell you the truth, up until last year, I had never even put up a tree at all. I mean, after all, I was one of those non-believers, one of the misguided people trying to get the nativities out of the town square and prayers out of any public place! But after what happened to me last year, and with your help, I renewed my faith and joined the church. For the first time in my adult life, I would like to put up a Christmas tree. Having a new house to decorate for the holidays in such a short amount of time might be difficult. If I buy this house, would you be able to help me get my house and tree decorated? You and the others—you know, Mary, Bonnie, Adriana, Ramon, and Maria. Could you all help me out?"

"You have come to the right place! Here in Sabal Palms, we go all out for the Christmas season! And everyone you named loves to prepare for the Christmas season."

"When I drove through town this morning, it looked like the whole town has been involved! I saw the decorations going up all over the town shops a week before Thanksgiving. Main Street just looks like home to me, my new hometown. It looks like a scene right out of a Christmas movie. It is quaint with the garlands and candy canes on each light post. And the manger, the big Christmas tree going up on Main Street this morning . . . It feels like home,"

"I'm delighted you feel that way! Ready to go look at this house? If you decide to buy it, I am positive Bonnie, Mary, and all the others will be more than happy to pitch in and decorate for you."

Trent opened the passenger door of his car for Elaine, and she settled in and fastened her seat belt. He maneuvered the car back onto the road into town.

"Where is this house you are considering?"

"Just around the corner from Adriana's house."

"Nice neighborhood. I think you will like it. It's quiet, mature gardens and palms trees, and usually, no alligators." She laughed.

"I remember the alligator tales after Jada hit!" he said.

"Yes, they kind of got out of their normal habitat for a few weeks. You heard about Bonnie's attempt to get a closeup picture of the alligator in town?"

He laughed. "I did."

"But they are now mostly back in their home resacas and lakes."

In no time, Trent pulled in front of a beautiful, light brown stucco house with Palm Beach Mission Spanish tile roof. The front yard was full of lovely tropical plants, including a bed with orange bird of paradise plants, banana plants on the sides of the house, and ferns lining the walkway. The outskirts of the front yard displayed queen palms, royal palms, and a Mexican fan palm tree. Orange marmalade shrubs were on one side of the courtyard. Inside, the courtyard held a variety of tropical plants; and in the corner, a small avocado tree, a lime tree, and a lemon tree took up about a third of the courtyard.

"My, this is very lovely, Trent. And look, on the other side of the house, in the shade, you have some healthy-looking red poinsettias, and along that back fence, white poinsettias. You have Christmas already blooming!"

"I had no idea until I came to Sabal Palms that the poinsettias can grow in flower beds here. Yes, I liked this house the first time the realtor showed it to me."

"I believe the Andersons lived here. Transferred for work, I heard."

"That is what the realtor told me as well."

They exited the car and walked up a wide Saltillo-tile walkway to the expansive front porch. Ceiling fans slowly whirred on the oversized front porch that spilled into a courtyard full of plants and a fountain on the side of the house. As they reached the door, the realtor opened the solid mahogany door before Trent could ring the bell.

"Come in, Trent. Hello, Elaine. Good of you to come on such short notice."

Elaine smiled. "Edna, good to see you."

"Nice to see you, too. Come inside and look around. Trent has been through the house a few times and knows his way around. Oh, and be sure to see the pool out back and the outdoor kitchen."

Trent guided Elaine throughout the large three-bedroom, three-bath house with an updated expanded living and kitchen area. He eagerly showed Elaine the backyard with all the features. He chattered on about each detail, and Elaine sensed how much Trent loved the house and the idea of living in it.

Trent gestured toward the pool, outdoor sitting area, and beach umbrella over a wrought iron table. "I can just see myself sitting out here by the pool and reading one of your books, Elaine. And over here"—he walked to the outdoor kitchen—"we can gather with the whole gang and have a cookout. And if it is chilly on a winter night, a firepit right over here."

"This is a wonderful backyard, Trent. You could host, perhaps, thirty people or more easily."

Trent continued the house tour and showed Elaine the inside closet space, an oversized pantry with a stained glass decorative door. He pointed out a large laundry room with built-in shelving, a rod for hanging clothes, a table for folding clothes, and a built-in ironing board. The bathrooms were extra-large, and every bedroom had walk-in closets. The large living room spilled into an oversized kitchen with a breakfast nook. A large, separate dining room was to the side for hosting more formal gatherings.

"Trent, this house has a multitude of unique features and plenty of living space."

"Let's step outside for a moment."

Trent took Elaine back out by the pool, away from Edna's ears, and asked, "What do you think of the place?"

"Trent, it is perfect. But what means more to me is that you are very happy with it, and you see yourself living here. Will it need inspection or repairs?"

"No. Not required for a cash purchase. I will have it inspected later and fix anything that is needed."

"Then it sounds like you are ready to go."

Trent beamed. "I am. Thank you, Elaine, for coming with me to see it."

"Trent, you know word of this purchase will be all over town by noon tomorrow. Adriana already suspects something is up. She heard you went to Edna's office the other day."

He laughed. "Don't worry. I intend to spill the beans myself. I want to let Mary, Bonnie, and Adriana know as soon as possible."

"Okay. You know what? This evening, we're decorating Bonnie's tree. We are meeting at five. Want to stop by? It would be the perfect time to tell them before they hear it anywhere else."

"That sounds like a good idea. Now, wait until I get there before you talk about it."

"Your secret is safe with me. I want to witness the looks on their faces when they hear the news!"

He laughed again. "We'd better get going. I'll take you back to your cottage. As for me, I believe I have some papers to sign at Edna's office." He winked at Elaine and then stopped inside the house to let Edna know he had made his decision. "I'll take it. How soon can I sign the deal?"

"Meet me back at the office in thirty minutes? I just need to lock up here and drop a 'For Sale' sign off on another property."

"Will do. See you in thirty minutes, Edna."

# Chapter Six

Elaine put Bella's dinner in a baggy and sealed it to take with her to Bonnie's house. The excitement Elaine felt was not just for decorating Bonnie's tree and enjoying Bonnie's famous Green chili chicken dinner; but most of all, she was eager to witness Trent's surprise visit to relay his news about buying a house in Sabal Palms.

"Come on, girl. We're going to drive over to Bonnie's house today with this big bowl of berries for dessert and bags of chips for the Green chili chicken. Let's get you in the car."

Elaine felt Bella's fluffy beard tickle her ankles all the way down the steps to the car. "Guess you're excited, too." She placed the berries in the front seat floorboard before fastening Bella in the back seat. "There you go."

The late afternoon sky displayed only a few light clouds and the warm December sun when Elaine drove her car down the small, beachside road. She turned the car along the crushed shell driveway and saw Mary pulling in behind her in her rearview mirror.

Elaine unfastened Bella from the back seat. "Come on, Bella, let's get up Bonnie's steps. You know the way. Atta girl. I'm right behind you with the food."

"Hello, there." Mary waved.

"Hi, Mary. Ready for more decorating?" Elaine asked.

"Of course! It's already the second day of December! We have much to do before the parties begin next week."

Elaine nodded. "Yes, Bella and I look forward to the coming festivities, don't we, girl? Let's get inside out of this heat."

Mary fanned her hands rapidly in front of her face to cool off a bit. "It's so hot for this time of year and this time of day. My goodness!"

"It is. Even Bella thinks it is hot."

Mary smiled. "She does have on a fur coat after all!"

"She sure does. Can I help you get anything from your car?"

"No. I brought some healthy breads for us to have with dinner. Just one basket to grab."

As Elaine and Mary made their way up the steps to Bonnie's cottage, Bella toddling behind them, Adriana's car screeched into the driveway.

"There she is." Mary chuckled. "Late as usual."

"Technically not late but the last to arrive," Elaine noted.

"You always see the bright side, Elaine."

"Try to, Mary." She winked.

"Girls, girls, girls! Oh, my goodness! You will never guess who is following me. It looked like Trent Fortune's car. I got just ahead of him at the light before the highway. It looks like he is coming this way. I figured he might be coming to see you, Elaine."

"Not expecting him to come to my house today," Elaine honestly stated.

Bonnie opened the front door of her beach cottage. "What is all this hollering?"

"Oh, it's Adriana," Mary said, "overexcited about something. Trent, I think."

"About what?" Bonnie asked.

"I saw Trent coming out this way. Just wondered if he was coming to see Elaine, but she said she wasn't expecting him at her house," Adriana gushed.

"Oh, for heaven's sakes, you all! Stop all that hollering!" Bonnie beckoned. "Get in here. I am letting all my cool air out."

Elaine remained silent on the subject of Trent's anticipated visit, but inside, she was about to burst to tell the girls.

Bonnie took the food from Elaine, and Mary proceeded to set out the other side dishes and chili bowls for a buffet-style dinner. Just as she had placed everything in the correct spot, her doorbell rang.

"Now what?" Bonnie asked.

Adriana leaped off the sofa with anticipation. "Oh, Bonnie, want me to get the door for you?" Before Bonnie could answer, Adriana was at the front door.

"Thank you," Bonnie said from the kitchen.

"My goodness, look who is here, ladies," Adriana said, opening the door.

"Hello, Trent," Elaine said.

"Ladies, good to see you all."

"Trent, I thought you might have been coming this way," Adriana remarked. "I noticed your car behind me on the road."

Bonnie hurried to the living room and gestured to the sofa. "Please come on in, Trent. What brings you this way? Are you hungry?"

Trent stepped into the living area. "May I sit?"

"Of course. May I get you something to drink? We're about to have dinner, and you are more than welcome to join us."

"Bonnie, that is so sweet of you. I haven't had a home-cooked meal since, well, the last time I came over to Elaine's for dinner. I would like it very much. You're sure you have enough for a last-minute guest?"

"Oh, we always have more than we can eat." She laughed. "I'll get you a chili bowl and silverware. It's buffet-style."

"Thank you, Bonnie. But before we eat, I just wanted to tell you all the news."

Adriana's eyes became as large as saucers. She batted her long eyelashes and inched closer to Trent, hanging on his every word. "Do tell; do tell," she said as she motioned with her hands with each syllable she uttered.

"Okay. Here it is." Trent cleared his throat. "I bought a house today."

"What?" Bonnie shrieked from the kitchen.

"That's amazing! Wonderful!" Mary said.

Elaine smiled, observing her friends' reactions.

"I knew it! Elaine, didn't I say it yesterday? I knew it!" Adriana beamed.

"Yes, she did say that," Mary confirmed.

Trent laughed as the women talked all at the same time. "And," he interrupted, "when I signed the contract today, Edna talked with the sellers, and I was able to move the date of possession up a day. I take possession in three days."

"Three days? That soon?" Bonnie asked. "That is fantastic!"

"Where is it? On the island?" Adriana asked.

"No. It is around the corner from your house, Adriana, on Marlin Drive."

"Oh! Oh! Did you buy the Andersons' place?" Adriana asked with excitement.

"The very one. The light brown stucco that has a courtyard on the side."

"Oh! It is so beautiful! And it has a terrific pool, too. I have always loved that one. In fact, dear Antony—may he rest in peace"—she crossed her chest—"and I watched as they built that one. It is an outstanding house."

Mary chimed in, "And the yard! Those plants! Good gracious! It has a tremendous collection of vividly colored tropical plants in the front and on the sides. Oh, and I know a good yard service if you want the contact information. I will be happy to connect you with the tropical plant experts in town. They can help you do just about anything you want, like put in a butterfly garden or a place to attract Green Jays. Just name it."

"Thank you, Mary. Ladies, I came to ask you all about doing me a favor, if you don't mind."

"Name it, Trent," Bonnie shouted and placed Trent's bowl on top of the stack on the counter.

"Yes, Trent. What can we do?" Mary asked.

Elaine listened. She knew Trent was going to ask the others to help get his new house ready for Christmas in record time, and she knew the other women would be thrilled to be a part of this project.

"I've never decorated a house for Christmas."

"Never?" Bonnie blurted in a surprised tone. "Oh, sorry."

"As you all know, being a Christian is new to me. I haven't celebrated the season before, at least not as an adult. I don't have a tree, ornaments—not one single thing. I used to just put signs up at the office that said, 'Enjoy your holiday.' And I even expected my employees to work on Christmas Eve and Christmas afternoon."

Adriana gasped. "You didn't!"

"I did. I didn't understand the importance of the season and of His birth."

"I never understood why an employer would make employees work on Christmas," Mary admonished.

Elaine felt she needed to rescue Trent from this conversation. "Remember, Trent had a different vision of his life then before he came back to Christ."

"Yes. My life was pretty much all work and all money."

"Oh, I'm so sorry, Trent," Adriana pleaded. "I didn't mean anything by it. I had forgotten about the old you. I guess I am used to the new you."

Trent laughed. "Thank you. I am glad you have put the old me in the past. But you are right. After all, I have been born again. It is a new me."

The women all clapped and laughed.

"Good point," Bonnie remarked.

"We're glad you have turned your life around," Mary added.

"How can we help?" Elaine asked, already knowing the reply.

"I am hoping you can help me get ready for Christmas."

"Do you have decorating ideas?" Adriana asked.

"What theme of decorations do you want? Traditional? Beach?" Bonnie asked.

"Endangered species theme?" Mary asked.

"Themes? I hadn't realized there were themes for decorating." He laughed. "First of all, I need a tree. I'm going to go by the tree lot and see Ramon early tomorrow morning to pick one out. I'll ask him to hold it for me for a couple of days. The realtor provided me with a key to the garage, so I can store other items there I will need for decorating. The favor I want to ask is if you ladies, and also Ramon and Maria, would be willing to help me decorate the house."

"Of course!" Mary said.

Adriana gushed, "Absolutely love to!"

Bonnie nodded.

Elaine, always the organizer of the group, took the lead. "Well, ladies, what are your plans for the next couple of days? We are decorating Bonnie's tree today and Mary and Adriana's trees the next couple of evenings. Trent, do you prefer evening, or is during the day okay for decorating?"

"The day and time don't matter to me. I'll get the tree set up in the stand in the house the day I take possession, three days from now, and that is the day my furniture will be delivered. But while I am waiting for the access to the house, can you suggest places in town to pick out some ornaments and other things for the tree? I can store them in the garage until we are ready to decorate. I know I'll need lights and ornaments. Any other suggestions?"

Elaine pointed to the bottom of Bonnie's tree. "Might see about a tree skirt, you know, for the bottom. It covers the stand."

"Thanks. I wouldn't have remembered that until I got the tree in the stand." He laughed.

"Trent, as I remember from when the house was built, doesn't it have a twelve-feet ceiling in the main living room?"

"Yes, Adriana. It is a very high ceiling."

Adriana continued. "You will want an eight-feet tree minimum but might want to see if Ramon has a nine-or ten-footer. And doesn't the house have a fireplace?"

"Yes, a rather large stone one with a wide mantel."

"And stairs off the main hallway to the second floor?"

"Yes, it does. You know the house well."

"Then you will probably want to purchase several garlands to string across the mantel and up the railing of the stairs."

"Thank you, Adriana. Those are great ideas. I wouldn't have thought about garlands or decorating the mantel. I have seen it done, and it always looks nice. Any recommendations where I should purchase ornaments?"

Mary eagerly spoke up. "All of the little shops in town should have them. The Seashell Gifts Company has ocean and nautical ornaments—and a few wildlife ones, as well. Most of the other shops have more traditional ornaments. Oh, and the antique store out on the highway has some wonderful old ornaments made in Mexico."

All eyes turned to Bonnie, who suddenly was chuckling nonstop. She took a short breath from her giggles. "And"—she laughed—"I just happen to have some extra tinsel."

At this, the women all burst into laughter. Bonnie explained to Trent how she was tangled up to the point of being paralyzed on Elaine's deck the day before.

"Ha! I am sorry I missed that sight," Trent said. "I would like to have had a picture of that for fun!"

"I'm glad there is no evidence of the mess I was in! It was unbelievable being caught up in that itchy stuff! It was like wearing a jacket on a hot afternoon!" Bonnie stood up and returned to the kitchen. "Gave me a heat rash! Shall we eat?"

As Trent made his way to the kitchen, he said, "Let me know what day will work for you all."

"It will be such fun to decorate a brand-new home! It sounds wonderful, Trent, with the fireplace, staircase, and all," Bonnie said.

The group sat at the table inside and listened to Christmas songs, enjoying the fellowship and food.

"Oh, Bonnie! Your chicken chili is amazing!" Adriana exclaimed.

All heads nodded in agreement.

Trent looked at the women and said, "With all of you helping me, my house can be decorated in such a way that I know it will feel like home. I want to invite my parents to come visit and see the new house."

"Trent, it is wonderful that you are settling here in Sabal Palms," Elaine said. "I think your family will like it. And from what you told me before about your family, I know you are pleased to have them come and visit you here."

"Elaine, you recall my family history? And that my father and I weren't exactly on speaking terms for a while?"

"Yes, I remember."

The others listened intently as they ate.

"I have been able to reestablish my relationship with my father. He is older now and regrets the times he was, well, under the influence and aggressive to me and my mom. She forgave him, and so did I. But now, watching them as they are aging, I want to have a different relationship with them and see them more often."

Bonnie nodded. "I understand and know exactly what you mean. And I can tell you, from the perspective of a mother, there was nothing as wonderful to me in my whole life as when my own son found his faith that was lost to him for years. I know your parents will just be happy to spend time with you."

"I am praying for a good visit. I think it is going to be a fantastic Christmas. Oh, and I almost forgot to ask you all, are you helping at church on Saturday?"

"To put up the church tree and the manger?" Adriana asked.

"Yes."

"I wouldn't miss it," Elaine said.

"Me either. We all help out every year," Bonnie added.

"Great," he said.

"Ladies, tomorrow, Mary's house?" Adriana asked.

Bonnie nodded. "And then your house after that, Adriana."

Trent smiled. "That means, the day I close on my house, you would all be free to decorate my tree?"

Adriana jingled her bracelets as she placed her hand on Trent's arm. "Of course."

"It's set, then," he said.

# Chapter Seven

Elaine felt the heaviness in her legs as she plodded up the steps to her deck holding the empty fruit bowl. The group at Bonnie's was so excited about Trent's news they all stayed later than usual. Bonnie's Christmas tree looked terrific. And Adriana could not stop telling the construction details about when she and Antony watched Trent's house being built many years ago.

"Bella, come on, girl. It's late, pooch. We've had a very long day."

Bella joined Elaine at the door just as the key turned the lock. A sudden blast of cool air out of the south caught her attention. She looked toward the island and saw thunderstorms flashing in the distance over the water. Each flash of lightning displayed the height of the tall thunderhead clouds. The bolts struck down to the water, reminding Elaine of the night Trent's plane had crashed and how he had changed since that near fatal accident.

"Oh, Bella. We'd better get inside before the storms blow our way. Come on, girl. I know. I'm tired also, Bella. But the day isn't over. I need to write a little bit."

Elaine's eyes followed Bella, who wasted no time listening to Elaine finish her sentence. The pup darted through the living room and into the bedroom to her little, fuzzy bed.

"Yeah. That looks like the best idea."

Elaine locked up the cottage, got ready for bed, and decided it would be best to wait until she was more rested to work on her children's Christmas book. The bed felt unusually wonderful as she slid between the sheets and turned off the lamp. But her mind would not rest. Pleasant thoughts about Christmas plans, decorating, and preparing for parties were unexpectedly interrupted by the feeling, the distinct realization, that she was being called to help someone. She sensed it in her heart and soul. Her heart told her God wanted her, Elaine Smith, to actively participate in bringing someone to Christ. Not in a passive way. Not the way she felt most comfortable: writing. She believed her writing was a ministry of sorts, achievable from her own comfortable writing space in her own comfortable cottage.

God had blessed her with a gift of writing, and she turned right around and hoped to praise and glorify Him with her work. Christian writing conveyed a message to the reader. Elaine wasn't required to speak directly to a person. A reader received a message through her writing, understood the meaning, and then, God helped the reader along the rest of the way.

She had spent her years since retirement writing books and stories for all ages. She had written devotionals and stories that had helped others in the past. She had written children's picture books and lyrics for Christian songs that might guide others to Christ. But she had never had to confront them face-to-face. Instead, God used her work to reach out to lost souls. That was how she had planted seeds of faith in Cara, the runaway teenage girl who had come back home; in Jack, the lost son of her best friend, Bonnie; and in Billy, who had returned to God and used his musical talent to reach others through Christian songs and worship music.

In the past, God had not required her to confront anyone face-to-face to witness and bring them to Him. He had assisted in that department. Through Elaine's writing, God had reached a former Mafia hitman in New York. God could reach anyone any time anywhere. God knows how to get people's attention through books, songs, or other means. God had used a storm to bring down Trent Fortune's plane last year, and then Jesus Himself had come to Trent in a vision. God did the heavy lifting, and Elaine was merely available to hear Trent's encounter and renewal of faith. But Elaine had not confronted any of these individuals nor asked them about their faith. They all read her work and came to her. Even Trent was aware of Elaine's Christian writing before his plane crashed. Now, she was being asked to approach someone first, face-to-face.

This felt different. Confronting someone required the vulnerability of possibly being rejected or criticized. Personal confrontation meant risk. It meant being uncomfortable and feeling nervous or anxious. The overwhelming feeling that she was being called to speak with a person was so intense, it kept her from sleeping, even though she was completely exhausted. Her mind wouldn't stop. She tossed and turned trying to find a position in which she could relax.

A clap of thunder startled her. Her heart raced. She was uneasy, and she felt the pain, the heartache someone was feeling at that very moment. She knew exactly who the person was. She had known it from the beginning, from the first time she had seen him. She knew when she saw his sad eyes. And now, she felt directed to reach out. She believed God was directing her to help Chris. Face-to-face.

Elaine's concerns deepened after Bonnie's report of his behavior at the coffee shop. If Chris was attempting to deal with his depression and grief by drinking, he was screaming for help. She knew she must act as soon as God directed her in the right direction. Whenever she was in doubt as to what to do, she returned to the one true Source for guidance: the Word of God.

She switched the light back on and took her Bible from the night table. As always, Elaine surrendered and opened her will to God. She would do as He wanted. "Okay," she whispered, looking upward, "lead the way."

Another clap of thunder and loud swishing of wind against her cottage startled Bella, who sat up, looked at Elaine, and laid back down.

Elaine flipped open her Bible. She wondered, how did others in biblical history know it was God calling? How did they know He was sending them forth to intervene on someone's future? And how would this relate to talking with Chris in the small town of Sabal Palms?

She decided to simply close her eyes and let her finger open the pages to see where God might lead her. She enjoyed this strategy when she wasn't certain where to start. The first verse opened to her was in the Old Testament. Elaine read from Isaiah 55:11, "So shall my word be that goes out from my mouth; it shall not return to me empty, but it shall accomplish that which I purpose, and shall succeed in the thing for which I sent it."

*My goodness*, she thought, *speaking on God's behalf is a lot of responsibility.* And then, she remembered she was only to plant the seed, and God would do the watering and feeding as needed. But she needed courage. She certainly didn't have the courage Isaiah had when he was first approached by God. She remembered the story and looked it up.

And there it was in Isaiah 6:8. Isaiah didn't hesitant when asked who would speak to the people on God's behalf; he volunteered to speak for God. "And I heard the voice of the Lord saying, 'Whom shall I send, and who will go for us?' Then I said, 'Here I am! Send me.'"

A sense of nervousness came over her. *This is crazy*, she thought. *It is eleven o'clock at night, and I am in bed. Why am I nervous about seeing Chris at some point in the future?*

She thumbed through the Bible, and it fell open to Acts, chapter ten. It was interesting that she was taken to verse forty-two: "And he commanded us to preach to the people and to testify that he is the one appointed by God to be judge of the living and the dead."

Elaine knew this verse spoke to judgment, accepting Christ, and knowing judgment is not meant to come from people but only from God. This verse puzzled her. How might a verse like this one relate to someone who needed help? She wondered if Chris was concerned about being judged, or perhaps, he had blamed someone for the death of this wife. *No way to fully know tonight*, she thought. She felt she was meant to see the verse, and it would have meaning for Chris. But tonight, she would pray about it and leave it to God to help her figure it out when the time came. He would guide her.

She knew she must follow God's lead. She remembered what had happened to Jonah when he refused God's direction to go to Nineveh. *I sure don't want to end up in the belly of a fish.* She laughed to herself.

Elaine looked at Bella, already snoozing in her little bed. She turned off the light and prayed until she fell asleep.


A loud knocking announced Bonnie was probably at Elaine's front door.

"Elaine, you up?" Bonnie yelled, knocking again on Elaine's door.

Elaine opened her door. "Yes, I'm up. You're here early for our walk. Come in. Let me get my shoes on."

"Okie dokie pokie. Yes, I was so excited to tell you I got a voice message last night from Chris." And without so much as a breath in between words, Bonnie, clearly enthused, continued. "Well, he left the message last night after midnight, so of course, I was already asleep and didn't listen to it until this morning. Wanted to tell you first thing. I think it will all work out."

Elaine tied her other shoe and stood up. "What did he say? And did he sound better than he did at the coffee shop?"

"He sounded okay. But it was a short message, so not sure. He said his tour boat is one of the boats in the boat parade, and he gave me a number to call about tickets."

"Well, that is exciting."

"Yes, I thought so, too."

Elaine took her key to lock up the cottage. "Bella, let's go, girl."

The trio left the cottage and began their routine walk along the shore toward the church.

"And Chris gave me a different number to pass along to Billy about the music for the parade. I'll tell the others about the tickets when we go to Mary's later today to help her with her tree. And speaking of decorating, how about the news Trent gave us last night? That was something. Buying a house here and asking us to help with decorating the entire house for Christmas in just a few days. And it's so large, who knows what we can do in just a few days? I hope he will buy everything he needs. And of course, there is the outside to decorate. And—"

"Bonnie, how much coffee *have* you had this morning?"

"Oh, two cups, sorry. Just excited and happy about Trent's news and the possibility of going on the boat parade."

"I'll admit it will be terrific to have Trent as a resident of Sabal Palms. It is pretty amazing. Are you familiar with the house he is buying?" Elaine turned to find Bella scurrying behind.

"I haven't been inside. I know where it is and love the courtyard. You know, we could ask him if he wants the courtyard decorated for Christmas, too."

"Excellent idea."

Bonnie stopped in her path on the sand, took a breath, and turned to Elaine. "Now, tell me the truth, Elaine. Did you know he was buying a house when Adriana mentioned Trent going to the realtor's office?"

Elaine laughed. "No, I didn't know it then."

"You didn't seem a bit surprised at the news."

"Trent told me later on, after Adriana had mentioned it."

"And you didn't tell us?"

"He wanted to tell everyone himself. I promised I wouldn't mention it."

"You sure kept a secret, all right. Okay, let's pick up the pace. The tide just went out, and I know we will see some great shells on our walk this morning."

Bella ran ahead and chased off a sandpiper from the edge of the water. She trotted back again and followed at Elaine's heels.

Elaine and Bonnie chatted all the way to the church on the shore and back to Bonnie's cottage.

"Well, Elaine, I'll see you later this afternoon. Looking forward to decorating Mary's tree."

"I'll come by around 4:30 to pick you up. I'm taking the salad this time."

"And I made a batch of sugar-free cookies. See you later."

Elaine and Bella returned to the cottage, and Elaine took a second cup of coffee out to the deck. "Aw, Bella, there sure is no better view than looking out over the water and watching the shorebirds in the morning."

Bella wagged her tail and laid down on the deck.

Elaine watched the brown pelican's straight vertical dive down to retrieve its breakfast. The Roseate Spoonbills walked along the shore looking for tasty bites. This was where she felt the most at peace, near to God and His creations.

The phone buzzed in her pocket, interrupting her thoughts.

"Hi, Billy."

"Good morning, Elaine. Is today a good day to work on the lyrics for the Christmas album?"

"Today? Yes, come on by."

"Great. My day is free. Need anything from town before I head out?"

"No. Thank you for asking. We can work most of the day. My only commitment is going to Mary's house later this afternoon to decorate her Christmas tree."

"I'll be there in maybe about thirty minutes. Elaine, how about I bring some lunch with me? We can work straight through. I'll stop at the deli."

"Perfect. I love their Reuben."

"Two Reubens it is. I'll call it in so it will be ready for me to pick up. See you in a few minutes."

Bella, relaxing in the sun, hopped up as soon as Elaine left her chair.

"Sorry for the interruption, Bella, but I need to get a salad made before Billy gets here. Let's go back inside. Don't have much time."

Faithful Bella turned her head and listened, followed Elaine inside, and found her little bed by the sofa.

# Chapter Eight

Billy arrived precisely thirty minutes after he phoned Elaine. Thankfully, she finished preparing the salad and was free for the day until time to depart for Mary's decorating gathering.

"Come in, Billy. I'm pleased you were able to come to Sabal Palms earlier than expected." Elaine took the to-go bag with the Reuben sandwiches to the kitchen. "I'll set these in here until we are ready to eat."

"Guess who I saw leaving the deli?"

"No clue."

"Chris.

"Did you get to talk to him about the boat parade?"

"No. He was driving off. Had a Christmas tree in the back of his truck. I guess he was delivering it for someone."

"I was hoping you could have asked him about music for the boat parade."

"That would have been a great opportunity. I waved at him, but he just pulled out from the parking lot onto the street. He was driving a little erratic."

"Oh?"

"Not sure how to explain it, but I was afraid he was going to hit another car passing by. But he made it out okay."

"I'm worried about him. I think he might need our prayers. But I tell you what. I am beyond excited about your getting to Sabal Palms this early before Christmas."

"Believe me, I was ecstatic to get down here earlier than planned. I needed to get out of Nashville for a while. Life gets very crazy over there sometimes. Busy. And lots of demands for my time. I was away from Sabal Palms for, let's see, almost four months this time. That album took longer than I thought it would. I believe it's because two of the songs are duets and we were required to work around the other vocalist's schedule."

"Oh? Are the two songs ones you and I wrote together?"

"Yes, and I believe you will be as pleased with the outcome as I am. The singer's name is Hana Lily Brown."

"Oh! Seriously? I love her voice! She is very beautiful, too. I'm thrilled she is the one you asked to sing the duets. And she is popular. I'll bet she has more requests for performances than you can count."

The more Elaine talked about Hana Lily Brown, the more Billy's expression changed. He looked down, avoiding eye contact, as his face turned crimson.

Elaine recognized that look. It was the look a young man has when he is completely smitten about a woman. "Billy, just wondering, are you, um . . . dating her?"

He looked at Elaine and replied, "Nothing official. Really. But I sure do enjoy her company. She seems to feel the same way, and we are staying in touch over Christmas. And the best part is her faith. She is a committed Christian. She told me her purpose in life is to use her voice to help others grow in their own faith."

"That is amazing. I heard her first songs on the Christian radio station before anyone else played her music."

"Yes. Her songs have crossed over to pop stations and even some middle-of-the-road contemporary music. But, Elaine, I would like to keep this just between us. No one is supposed to know about her singing on the album until we are ready for the release. And I especially want to keep it quiet about us, you know, seeing each other."

"Promise."

Billy looked directly at Elaine with worried eyes. "I can just imagine how Adriana might get overly excited about a potential romance."

"I promise. Mum's the word. Oh, Billy, I almost forgot to tell you."

"Tell me.!"

"Bonnie talked to Chris, the boat tour captain, about the Christmas boat parade. She wanted me to tell you she has a number for you to call about music for the tourist boat."

"Perfect. I'll give her a call."

"Good. Hope it works out for you to play on the boat. Now, how about your ideas for Christmas songs? Would you like coffee while we work?"

"Coffee sounds good. Let's get started."


Billy and Elaine made headway on writing a new Christmas song. They took a short break for lunch, then worked until 3:30. "I hate to stop when we are on a roll, Billy, but I should be getting ready to go to Mary's house."

"No problem. I believe we made outstanding progress today, as usual. You're so quick with writing lyrics. I will work a little more on the melody tonight. Can we meet same time tomorrow?"

"That works for me. We can work another five or six hours. I'll fix a lunch ahead of time for us."

"Thanks, Elaine."

She locked the cottage door and prepared to go to Mary's house. "Can't go looking like this, Miss Bella."

Bella tilted her head and followed Elaine around her room as she changed clothes. "Don't worry, you are going with me. Mary always welcomes you."

Bonnie was locking her front door when Elaine pulled into her driveway. She hustled down her steps and to Elaine's car.

"Hey, you two," she exclaimed to Bella and Elaine. "I am ready for this party. I believe our group has this decorating thing down to an art."

"I agree. It seems to take us less time each year."

"Not last night, with Trent's news. It was exciting, though."

Elaine and Bonnie turned into Mary's driveway and saw Mary beckoning from the porch before Elaine put the car in park.

"Look at her," Bonnie said. "She looks as frantic as Bella did this morning when that crab swiped at her nose."

"Wonder what's up."

Elaine and Bonnie took their dinner contributions up to the porch as Mary shouted, "Get up here! I have news!"

"We are here already, for goodness' sake!" Bonnie said. "What is all the hoopla?"

"I ran into Chris this afternoon at the gas station. He said we are in for the boat parade. We can all get tickets with his tour boat."

"Really?" Bonnie asked.

Adriana, last to arrive, pulled her car up to Mary's driveway, parked, and hopped out of the sportscar.

"About time," Bonnie yelled.

"Yeah! Get up here! Great news!" Mary hollered.

Stepping out in her strappy sandals and bejeweled arms, she shrugged her shoulders. "Why? Did I miss something?"

"Yes, get up here," Mary fussed and gestured rapidly.

Adriana took a tray of appetizers from her back seat and slammed the door. "Okay, I'm coming already. My stars, what's the uproar?" Adriana was clearly frustrated that she was not able to wave her arms about as she talked. Her fashionable, high-heeled shoes clicked up the sidewalk and the steps to the porch.

"The uproar is," Mary said, "we're in!" Mary jumped up and down on the porch clapping her hands, which sent her turtle earrings swinging back and forth until they nearly popped off her ears. "We are going on the boat parade next week! We're in!"

"Well, that's just fabulous!" Adriana spurted. "Oh, my heavens! That is wonderful! Let me set these stuffed jalapeños in the kitchen."

The women followed Adriana, and all placed their dinner creations on Mary's kitchen counter next to a fresh bouquet of white and pink plumerias from her yard.

Bonnie couldn't wait another second. "Spill it, Mary. Tell us the details. What did Chris say? How does it work? What time do we board the boat?"

Adriana jumped in, clanging her bracelets as she talked as much with her hands as her voice. "What should we wear? Casual okay? Dressy casual, I mean. Will that work?"

"Oh, hold your horses! First, I saw Chris at the gas station—"

"You said that already. Mary, please tell me you didn't forget you already mentioned that. Goodness, you are too young to have . . . slippage," Bonnie teased.

"No, of course not. I remember that I told *you* I saw Chris, but I hadn't yet told Adriana."

"Bonnie, let her finish," Adriana admonished.

"Okay, tell us the rest already," Bonnie pushed.

Mary turned to Bonnie. "Chris told me he gave you the phone number for Billy to call about the music."

"Yes, I did talk to Billy earlier today," Bonnie affirmed.

Mary continued. "Right. Okay, so here is what happened next. Billy followed up and called Chris. Chris gave Billy the phone number of his boss. And Billy called Chris's boss, who later told Chris he hired Billy to sing for the whole evening.

"Slow down! My head is spinning!" Adriana shrieked.

"Okay. Have you followed?" Mary asked.

"I think so," Adriana said. "Basically, Billy called the boss, who hired him?"

"Well, that is certainly easier to understand," Bonnie said.

"Fiddlesticks! But here's the best part," Mary continued. "Billy refused to take any money for the job. Instead, he asked about the Christmas boat parade. And the boss agreed and said we are all welcome."

"My lands!" Adriana squealed. "Bless Billy's heart for thinking of all of us! Just as sweet as my dear Antony, God rest his soul." As always, she followed this with the crossing of her chest.

"Billy has a big heart," Elaine noted.

Adriana gushed once again. "Billy arranged that for us *all*? How wonderful." She waved her bejeweled hands in the air. "Oh my, I hope that won't cut into their profits."

"I asked Chris about that when I saw him today," Mary said, "and he laughed. He said the boat holds over a hundred people, and it won't be a problem. Oh, and Chris said he is going to be the captain that night for the parade!"

"That's great news! Maybe we can get to know him a little better," Bonnie said.

Elaine recalled her feelings the night before about Chris. She knew she would need to pray for guidance before she saw him on the boat. She knew God would provide her with an opportunity to speak to him in the future. If not on the night of the boat parade, maybe another Christmas event.

Once the excitement about the parade subsided, the group began decorating Mary's Christmas tree and enjoyed a potluck dinner. Listening to Christmas music every night with her friends enhanced Elaine's feeling of the Christmas spirit. After the decorating of Mary's house was completed, Elaine and Bonnie returned to their cottages on the beach.

Billy and Elaine worked most of the day on the second Christmas song for the new album. Elaine walked Billy to the door, then quickly dressed for another tree-decorating party. The women met at Adriana's house, enjoyed another meal together, and helped Adriana with her tree and mantel. They decorated outside the house, hanging lights along the fence around the pool.

Mary and Bonnie volunteered to assist with kitchen clean-up duties after dinner.

"Elaine, let's check out front once more."

Elaine and Adriana walked onto her large front porch.

"This is my favorite part, decorating the outside." Adriana sighed and looked upward. "Antony was always in charge of this part—God rest his soul." She crossed her chest.

"This looks wonderful, Adriana. Antony would be proud. Want to check out back as well?"

Once Mary and Bonnie had completed their kitchen duties, they joined Elaine and Adriana in the backyard.

Adriana looked over the pool lights as they twinkled and were reflected in the pool water. "It looks just amazing! I do wish poor Antony—God rest his soul—was here to see it. He always loved hanging around the pool."

Elaine placed her arm around Adriana. "I am sure Antony knows how festive it looks."

"I know. I just miss him after all these years, all these Christmases. If it wasn't for you all, I would feel just plain sad. But getting together really helps."

Elaine looked her in the eye and, to comfort her, said, "Adriana. I think we all feel the same way. Holidays are harder when we have a loved one who is in Heaven. But we look out after each other now."

Adriana gasped and looked at Elaine. "Oh, Elaine, what about poor Chris? It's his first Christmas since his wife passed away."

"I thought about that last night. I'm worried about Chris. Let's make an effort to include him in Christmas activities. He might be ready to be around people."

Adriana nodded. "Yes, Elaine. We must. He can tell us if he is ready to go to such events. I know it took me a while, but later, I needed to be around people."

"I was the same way," Mary added. "He will be better eventually."

Elaine glanced at her watch. "Bonnie, I guess we'd better go back to the beach. Don't want to be out as late as we were last night."

"Okay. I'll retrieve our dishes from the kitchen."

Elaine, Bonnie, and Mary gathered their pans and casserole dishes from Adriana's kitchen.

"Ladies," Adriana said, "thank you once again for all your help getting my house ready."

"You're welcome. Now, tomorrow," Elaine said, "we will help Trent with his new house. He asked me if we could meet over there around four. His furniture is being delivered in the morning. I think it would be a good idea to take dinner over for him."

Adriana clapped her hands and said, "We must!"

"Want me to text you all and plan out a menu tomorrow morning?" Mary asked.

"That would be a big help," Bonnie said. "No sense in us all taking a green salad."

Adriana laughed and halfway snorted, then gasped, and snorted again. "Oh, excuse me! No, it wouldn't work if we all showed up with the same thing."

# Chapter Nine

The next morning, Elaine contacted Mary, Adriana, and Bonnie and suggested an impromptu planning meeting was needed at the coffee shop to brainstorm ideas about decorating Trent's house. There was no question the women were excited about the idea of decorating Trent's brand-new house from scratch. It was not only a newly purchased house, but also, Trent had never decorated for the Christmas season. They wanted Trent to have a memorable experience for his first Christmas in his new home.

Elaine honked her horn for Bonnie, who promptly exited her cottage and zipped down her steps to the car.

"Good idea to meet this morning, Elaine," Bonnie said as she plopped in the front seat of Elaine's car. "We don't want to be running around Trent's house looking like chickens with our heads chopped off!"

"That is a gruesome visual." Elaine laughed.

"You know what I mean."

"Yes. Don't want to be completely disorganized."

Bonnie turned up the volume on the car radio. "Oh, I love these old carols."

"Me, too. I especially love the songs about the birth and the wonder of it all," Elaine said, humming along with the tunes.

Before long, Elaine and Mary were singing the songs along with the choirs and vocalists on the radio.

Elaine parked the car on Main Street near the coffee shop.

"Look, Elaine, Mary's car. She beat us."

"She lives closer."

"By that logic, Adriana should be here, too," Bonnie retorted.

Alexa looked up at the jingle of the bell on the door. "Good morning, Elaine, Bonnie. The usual?"

Simultaneously, both women nodded and said, "Yes, please."

Elaine noticed the garlands, twinkle lights, glass ornaments, and a manger atop the back of the coffee bar. Flameless candles were set on each table. A snow globe sat on the counter by the cash register. "Bonnie, look at these decorations. Alexa, did you do all the decorating?"

Alexa beamed. "Yes. The owner gave me a small budget to fix it up. I worked on it until midnight last night after I closed."

"Outstanding job," Elaine commended.

"Thank you. Glad you like it. Cheers me up during my time at work."

Bonnie said, "I'll bet. It is wonderful. The shop looks even cozier than usual."

From across the room, Mary called out loudly, "Ladies, good morning. Grab your coffees and come on over. I already jotted down some notes."

The three were situated at the table when Adriana entered in a long, flowered skirt; bright pink blouse; and white, tissue-paper-thin sweater. "Alexa! Good morning! You know what I like."

"Caramel Macchiato with a double shot, extra whip?"

"Perfect. Oh, Alexa. I love what you've done with the place."

"Thank you."

Adriana, shoes clicking and jewelry clanking, joined the other women at the table. "Good morning, good morning! I am beyond excited! Beyond excited! Decorating a new house! Do you think Trent picked up all the items we suggested?"

"Good morning, Adriana," Elaine said. "Haven't talked to him since we gave him the list and the shops to visit for purchases. Ramon told me he delivered Trent's tree to him two days ago."

"That's a start," Mary stated.

"How should we proceed since we don't know the ornaments or other decorations?" Elaine asked.

Alexa brought Adriana's Macchiato to the table. "Here you go."

Adriana placed her hand on Alexa's wrist. "You are a dear. Thank you so much."

"No problem. Anyone need anything else?"

"Not me. Ladies?" Bonnie asked.

"I think we're fine," Elaine said. "Thank you."

Bonnie swallowed her coffee and said, "How about we toss around ideas for each room?"

"I like it," Adriana agreed. "We know he has a large living room with a fireplace, a sun porch, outdoor courtyard, and large entry and front porch."

"Hmm . . . " Bonnie frowned. "Sounds like a lot of space to consider."

Mary, who was known in town for her outside decorations on her porch as well as the interior, spoke up. "I would like to work on the outdoor space if that is okay with you. The porch, the courtyard, and—if he has enough decorations—the backyard by the pool."

Adriana chimed in, "I'll help you. I love doing the outside."

"Bonnie," Elaine said, "looks like you and I will do the inside rooms first, then. But what do you think about us first helping with the tree? Then we can concentrate on the other areas. Oh, and Adriana, when it comes time for the mantel and staircase, we might need you and Mary to supervise."

"Be happy to."

A jingle of the bell drew all eyes to the front.

"It's Chris," Bonnie said. "Must be on his way to the Christmas tree lot."

Chris ordered his coffee, turned to the ladies, and nodded. Each waved in return.

"Elaine, should we invite him to our parties?" Mary asked.

"Yes, as soon as we have the dates and times."

Chris took his coffee from Alexa and nodded again to the women.

"He looks lonely," Adriana observed.

"Hope we can help him with that," Bonnie said. "But after all, will he want to hang out with a bunch of old women?"

"Oh!" Adriana said. "Speak for yourself."

"Okay, three old women and one almost-old woman." Bonnie laughed.

Mary exclaimed, "We do look amazing for our age, you know?"

"I know I do." Adriana laughed.

Mary continued, "As I was saying, we look really good. I mean, have you seen—oh, what is her name . . . "

Elaine was anxious to get the women back on task and halt the gossip about to spurt from Mary about who she thought looked old. She nudged Mary with her elbow and pointed to the paper. "Which room should we discuss next?"

Mary turned the page of notes toward the other women to read. "Ladies, back to work. Here is what we have decided so far. Now"—she turned the page—"Adriana, can you sketch the rooms as you recall seeing them?"

"I saw the rooms a long time ago; it's been years."

Elaine felt she needed to help the women with the sketch for planning. "I have been inside the house."

Adriana turned. "What? When?"

"Well, remember I told you that I learned about Trent wanting to buy the house right before he purchased it?"

They nodded.

"I looked at the house with Trent right before he signed the contract. He asked me to go with him to see it. He wanted to get my opinion."

Bonnie shook her finger. "Ah ha! I thought so! You *did* know about the house."

"Yes, but after Adriana told us she saw Trent go into the realtor's office. I didn't know about it until later that day. And he asked me not to tell, remember?"

"It doesn't matter now," said Mary, redirecting the conversation. "What matters is we need to know how to decorate it. It is okay that you didn't tell us."

"Yes, after all, Trent did ask her not to tell anyone," Adriana affirmed.

"And I kept my promise."

"Yes, you did," Bonnie said. "So, sketch it, girl."

Elaine took the paper and pencil and said, "Okay, here is what I remember about the set-up of the living room. But it had no furniture the day we went to see it. Here is the fireplace and the entryway, and over here is the open kitchen. The stairway is over here. And this is the other door to the courtyard."

Elaine passed the paper around the table.

"Uh huh," Bonnie said.

"I see," added Mary.

"Okay," Adriana said. "It is *just* as I remember it when it was being built."

Elaine reached for the paper once again. "Now, ladies, where should we put things? I am guessing Trent might put the tree here by this large window. That is where I would want to put it. Suggestions for the rest of the room?"

The ladies continued the discussion until almost time for lunch when Adriana glanced at the clock and jumped up from her chair. "Well, ladies, gotta run. Have a mani-pedi scheduled. See you at Trent's?"

"Yes," Mary said, "I should get home to work on Trent's dinner for tonight. Need to stop at the store first."

"Bonnie, we should return to our cottages and get our side dishes ready, too."

"I'm ready." Bonnie stood and pushed her chair under the table.

# Chapter Ten

Bonnie, Elaine, and Mary arrived at Trent's house at the same time and found Adriana already going into Trent's front door.

"Would you look at that?" Bonnie observed. "She is early for once."

"She does live just around the block," Mary added. "But still, I'm surprised she's early."

"Looks like the girls are all here," Elaine said.

Seeing the women walking up the sidewalk as he let Adriana inside, Trent said, "Welcome! And you are all carrying dishes of food!"

Mary laughed. "And plenty of paper plates, drinks, utensils—you name it, we brought it. You know we are all about eating!"

"You got that right!" Bonnie said.

"I hadn't expected this! You ladies are wonderful! I was going to order a pizza. Come in and set those in the kitchen."

Elaine and the others placed their dinner dishes in the oven.

Gesturing toward the living area, stairway, and mantel, Adriana said, "Trent, we have plans for the décor."

"I am excited to see what you ladies can do with this place. Ramon and Maria are coming over, too, but are running late. He called and said he was swamped with customers at the tree lot."

Mary walked through the living room where the Christmas tree was placed in front of the large window. "In the window, just as we thought. This is the perfect place for the tree, Trent."

"Good. Now, here are some of the boxes and here, more boxes and over there, other boxes of decorations. I went to the shops on Main Street and a couple of places in Harlingen and found every item you suggested. I even added a few things from the antique store you mentioned. Just tell me what to do and where to start."

"My stars!" Adriana screeched. "You have been busy shopping!"

Elaine looked at her watch. "Dinner will be ready in about forty-five minutes. I think we can get a good part of the tree done by then if we all pitch in."

Bonnie opened the boxes of lights. "Let's start with these."

"I'll get the ladder to string the top of the tree and hang the decorations up there," Trent noted. "Oh, I almost forgot. I just put a new sound system in right over here. I'll start the Christmas songs before we begin."

Elaine smiled. "Now, with the little bit of cooler weather this afternoon, it is beginning to feel like the Christmas season!"

They continued the decorating, the women placing the decorations around the bottom and middle of the tree and Trent hanging the ones at the top. Just as predicted, forty-five minutes later, the dinner casseroles were ready. Elaine and Mary worked to get everything out of the oven and onto the oversized quartz counter for a buffet. They set places for all with the paper and plasticware on Trent's new breakfast table.

"Dinner break," Mary announced.

The group quickly assembled their individual plates and selected their drinks from the new double-sized refrigerator. One by one, they sat down in the breakfast nook area overlooking the pool in the backyard through the large bay window.

Between bites of dinner, Adriana complimented Trent's house. "Trent, I cannot believe this house. The pool, the oversized rooms and high ceilings, the detailed built-ins . . . I think it is a perfect match for you. I mean, it is large enough to entertain for business—"

"Or pleasure," Bonnie blurted. "We are happy to come over anytime."

Trent, with his mouth full of dinner, could only laugh and nod.

No sooner had dinner been consumed than the ladies all pitched in to clean Trent's kitchen.

"Back to decorating," Bonnie commanded.

At that moment, the doorbell rang. "Must be Ramon and Maria," Trent said. "I'll be right back."

Trent soon returned with Maria and Ramon following close behind.

Maria looked around the living area and said, "Oh, this house!"

Ramon shook hands with Trent. "Trent, good to see you. Looks like these ladies have it under control in here. Great house."

"Thank you. Want to take a quick tour?"

"I do," Maria said.

Trent took them throughout the house. At the end of the quick tour, Trent said, "And this is where the elves have been at work."

"I'll say. That tree certainly looks good there. And you're right. You needed a ten-feet tree."

The hours passed quickly. Trent, Ramon, and the women hummed and sang along to the music. The tree was adorned. Garlands were wrapped around the stair rail all the way up the stairs. Garlands were strung over the mantel, and stockings were hung. Strings of lights were placed around the house, inside and out. The courtyard had larger outdoor lights around the wall. All the while, songs about Christmas night, snow, bells, fireplaces, and candy—along with traditional Christmas hymns—were heard throughout the night.

At the end of the evening, Trent said, "Ladies and gentleman, it looks as if Santa's own elves were here decorating all day! No, I take it back. It looks like the elves and all the staff at the North Pole were decorating here today! This place looks amazing. I think you all know your stuff."

"It was enjoyable for us all," Elaine said.

"This was like nothing I have ever done before—decorating a brand-new house," Mary said.

"And you picked out some unique decorations." Adriana walked through the house, clicking her shoes on the tile floors in the kitchen, and gestured all around the house. "Look at these. Your personality really shines through with your choices. Just beautiful. And this one—oh my goodness. So delicate. Very well done, Trent."

"Agree one hundred percent," Mary noted.

"I especially like the handmade decorations and nativity from Mexico. Very nice," Maria said.

Bonnie yawned. "Excuse me. Elaine, I think we should be heading back out to the shore. You about ready?"

"You're right. Trent, see you in a couple of days?"

"For the boat parade?" he asked.

"Yes, but that morning, the church is putting up the tree if you're interested," Elaine replied. "Should be a festive day."

"Looking forward to it. And I would like to join at the church for decorating, also. What time?"

"Nine o'clock Saturday," Elaine replied.

"I will be at the tree lot," Ramon said. "But Pastor Sam knows he can call me if he needs something. I'm taking the tree over tomorrow."

"Ramon, how is Chris working out?" asked Elaine. "We've seen him around town, and something seems a bit . . . off with him."

"Yes, I've noticed it, too." Ramon shook his head sadly. "I'm keeping a close eye on him, and I've tried to get him to open up to me. But his grief is still fresh. I think we just need to pray for him."

The conversation turned back to decorating the church as the women filled in the details for Trent.

"Don't forget it starts at nine o'clock on Saturday," Mary said. "We will all be there."

"Sounds good," Trent said. "I wouldn't miss helping out at church. Will you all know the details about where the boat loads on Saturday? I need to know where we should park."

"Of course," Elaine replied. "I'll ask Billy tomorrow when he comes over. I believe the person who hired him gave him all the information, including parking and so on. I can send you the details. I think you will all enjoy Billy's songs. He is even going to play a couple of new tunes we have been working on this week."

"Seriously? New songs!" Adriana gasped. "Fabulous!"

The group walked to Trent's door, clean casserole dishes and bowls in hand.

"See you ladies day after tomorrow."

Mary, the last one out the front door, turned to Trent. "Good night, Trent. See you soon."

# Chapter Eleven

It was here—the day of decorating the church followed by the Christmas boat parade. This was the big event of the season for Elaine, Mary, Bonnie, and Adriana. This was the day they would attempt to have a new adventure for Christmas. It would be one for the history books, of that Elaine had no doubt. After their decorating tasks at church were completed, they would ride in the boat parade, and Billy Wrangle would debut two new Christmas songs. It would be a Christmas like no other.

"Let's go, Bella. We need to get our morning walk in and be back early today. Bonnie and I are expected to be at the church by nine o'clock."

Bella followed Elaine to the front door and exited right behind her. The chill in the air could not be denied. Further north, in the Midwest or Northwest, a temperature of sixty degrees was typical of some early summer afternoons and might find the Northerners and Midwesterners in shorts. But here on the coast of Texas, sixty-degree lows meant digging out long pants and long-sleeved shirts. For the acclimated residents of Sabal Palms, this was as close to an early winter temperature as could be expected. The afternoon would see temperatures in the mid-seventies—cool by coastal standards. Elaine was thankful she had decided on a lightweight jacket for her morning walk.

Elaine and Bella met Bonnie at her cottage steps. "Downright chilly," Bonnie said. "And that breeze! Brrr."

"Indeed. Good thing you have your sweats on."

"Yes, I first stepped out the door in my usual walking shorts a few minutes ago and had a change of heart." She grinned.

"Glad you switched. I'm thinking we should do a quick walk today."

Bonnie agreed. "Good thinking. I think I can wear my church-decorating attire for the entire day. This afternoon, after we are back from church, I'll take an extra jacket for the boat ride this evening."

"Think I will do the same. I forgot to check with Pastor Sam about lunch."

"Oh, I asked him yesterday at the coffee shop. He said the church ladies' council is providing lunch for the decorating committee again this year. So, no worries. We can take our time decorating and not have to fix lunch when we get home."

"Thanks, Bonnie. A week ago, I was not anywhere in the ballpark of being ready for Christmas."

"Ha, Elaine, I know what you mean. But the change in the weather the last few days has helped. And my goodness, everywhere we look—in town, on the streets, in our houses, in the shops—there are Christmas decorations galore! I think this is as close to looking like the North Pole as Sabal Palms could! Garlands are overflowing, wreaths on every door downtown, and each window has some kind of decorative display. It looks like the North Pole, for sure. Except, of course, no snow."

"And don't forget, there are no palm trees at the North Pole."

They both chuckled.

Bonnie shivered. "Hey, Elaine, ever notice how much faster we walk when it is cold?"

"We do; it's true. But when we turn back toward our cottages, we will be out of the wind."

"Good. Let's turn. I'm ready to be warmer!"

The women turned toward their cottages and felt the total absence of the wind.

"So much better," Elaine said.

"Yes, it is."

Approaching her cottage, Bonnie asked, "Pick me up to go to church? Don't want to walk all dressed up."

"Of course. In about an hour?"

"Okay."

Within minutes, Elaine was back at her cottage getting ready for the day's events. Elaine selected her white winter jeans; a long-sleeved, turquoise shirt; and a light-weight, white sweater. She would take another jacket on the boat ride.

Elaine noticed Bella following her every step. Bella seemed to sense when Elaine would be gone most of the day. "Bella, I'll be back in a little while. You take your morning nap."

Bella reluctantly went to her bed beside the sofa and sighed.

Elaine locked the cottage and drove to Bonnie's house.

"Ready for this?" Bonnie asked, closing her car door.

"I am. Ramon said the church ordered a taller tree this year. I'm glad Trent and Billy are coming to help. We will need them to climb up the ladder and decorate."

"Here we are. Looks like we are the first," Bonnie said.

"We are a couple minutes early. But I'll bet Pastor Sam has already opened the sanctuary."

Bonnie jumped from the car before Elaine turned off the engine. "Excited, Bonnie?"

Bonnie laughed. "Tis the season! Let's go see the tree."

Elaine opened the door to the sanctuary, where Sam was standing next to the enormous tree. "Isn't this a beautiful tree, ladies?"

"Oh, wow!" Bonnie exclaimed. "And the smell . . . my goodness."

"The evergreen smell fills the entire sanctuary. I don't believe we have had one this pretty in probably more than five years. Ramon picked a good one for us."

Elaine nodded. "He did indeed."

In the background, Christmas hymns could be heard. Elaine turned to see the source.

"Like that?" Pastor Sam asked. "I just added the sound system with speakers throughout the church. An anonymous donor made it possible." He winked at Elaine.

Elaine smiled and hoped Bonnie hadn't seen Pastor wink at her. Even Bonnie didn't know that Elaine donated her music royalties to the church on the shore. She wanted to keep it that way.

"The sound is lovely. Enhanced, I think."

Bonnie nodded. "It adds a lot, Pastor. You can feel Christmas in the air."

An opening of the door drew their attention to the back of the sanctuary to see Adriana and Mary, followed by Trent, Billy, and Maria.

"Looks like everyone is here," Pastor Sam said.

Billy stepped forward to Pastor Sam and shook his hand. "Pastor."

Trent followed and shook Pastor Sam's hand.

"Good to see you Billy, Trent, and all of you. I am so appreciative of your help today. Every year, you ladies come and do wonderful work for the church. It would not be possible without your help. And delighted to have Billy and Trent this year."

"We enjoy it very much," Elaine said.

"Thank you. It means a lot to me—and the congregation. Now, let's get started. Billy and Trent, there is a twelve-feet ladder in the side hallway. The maintenance man left it there yesterday, so we can get to the top. And the ornaments are in the storage closet just off my office. I need to do a few things in my office while you all are working. If you need anything, just knock on the office door. Ready to start?"

"Yes, sir," Trent said.

Immediately, the group scattered, each retrieving the needed items for the tree decoration assignment. The music filled the atmosphere and gradually, the tree, the altar, and the ends of the pews were adorned with ornaments, garlands, bows, and silk flowers. After three hours of non-stop work, the tree and the sanctuary were completed.

"Let's just step back," Elaine suggested, "and see how this looks as we enter church."

The group returned to the door of the sanctuary and examined the entire room.

Adriana gasped. "My heavens!"

"It is stunning," Maria said.

"Absolutely amazing," Trent agreed. "You all have skilled decorating techniques."

"And now"—Bonnie laughed—"the reward."

Trent, puzzled, asked, "Reward?"

Elaine laughed. "She is talking about a lunch prepared for us in the fellowship room."

"Ah, I see. I can always eat," Trent said.

"I'm all in," Billy piped in.

The group found a table full of delicious options displayed across a long table in the fellowship room. The ladies' church council stood ready to serve plates and pour iced tea and coffee. Pastor Sam introduced the tree decorators to the women in the council.

"The church sure knows how to treat helpers," Trent said. "This will be my new home church."

Elaine sat next to Trent. "Trent, have you told Pastor Sam about your move to Sabal Palms?"

"I haven't. Now is a good time, I think."

"Yes, he may have heard it in town, but it would be nice for you to talk to him all the same."

"I'll go sit beside him at his table. Looks like there is one chair open."

Adriana watched every move Trent made. She always wanted to know the latest news about everyone in town. "What's he doing?"

"He is telling Pastor about his new house. He wants the church to be his home church."

Adriana began waving her arms about. "That is marvelous! Just marvelous!"

Bonnie, Mary, and Maria continued eating.

"Guess those girls were hungry," Adriana teased.

"Me, too." Elaine stood up from the table. "Think I need a little more salad."

When everyone had finished lunch, they thanked the council for preparing the delectable meal, and each went to their own cars.

"Elaine, see you in a couple of hours," Billy said.

"Okay. Either as we are boarding or on the boat. I will look for you."

Mary and Adriana said their goodbyes.

Maria walked with Elaine in the parking lot. "Elaine, Ramon and I will see you later today on the boat. He is closing the Christmas tree lot early. Said he wouldn't miss it. And besides, he only has a few trees left."

"We will all see you both on the boat."

# Chapter Twelve

Elaine let Bella out one more time and then fed her dinner. She checked her hair once more, put on more lip gloss, and grabbed her jacket.

"Bella, see you in a bit. I promise it will be the last time I leave you today."

Elaine had to admit she felt guilty leaving the little pooch for so many hours on the same day. But Bella would be fine waiting for Elaine.

Bonnie plopped in the front seat and grinned from ear to ear. "Well, jeepers! This is it! I am so excited!"

Elaine laughed. "I have to say, I am, too. This is an adventure unlike our others."

"Yes, and Billy is going to introduce the new Christmas songs. How exciting!"

"And the weather is perfect. The wind is gone. It's clear. The temperature is holding at sixty-eight."

"You know what is one of the best things about being out on the boat at night?"

"Not really. I forgot you had a boat for a while years ago."

"We did. It was many, many years ago. But I still recall the stars. When you are out away from the lights and the water is still, the twinkling stars reflect on the water. And you can see so many more than when you are on land near lights."

"I am very anxious to see that sight! More of God's handiwork on display!"

Elaine drove over the two-mile causeway to the island. The sun was setting, and it reflected bright yellow, orange, red, and even purple in the water. "Will you look at this sunset!"

Bonnie took out her cell phone. "Need pictures of this one. I will send them to Jack. He'll be down in a couple of weeks. This will be a reminder of what he can see down here on his trip."

"You didn't tell me. How exciting. My kids will be here around that time, too. Such a great time of year to be with family."

"It is indeed. Oh, look, just up ahead. They are directing traffic. I think we turn in at the next parking lot to board the boat."

Elaine parked the car, and she and Bonnie walked toward the boat.

"Hey, girls!" Adriana called. "I picked up Mary, so we wouldn't have two cars to go home."

"She did. And we talked about being on a boat all the way over here," Mary said, tilting her head twice toward Adriana. Elaine knew Mary was communicating that Adriana was getting anxious, as Adriana had been known to do.

"This is going to be fun, right? You promise we aren't going out to sea? No rough water?" Adriana pleaded.

Elaine put her hand on Adriana's arm. "No, we are not going out to sea. You will see the lights on the shore the entire time. No open sea."

"Okay, I will hold you to that," she said anxiously. She grabbed Elaine's hand and squeezed, then put her arm in Elaine's.

Elaine walked arm-in-arm with Adriana. "Let's go. I think Billy is already aboard. Trent may be as well."

"Okay," Adriana agreed. "Let's go find them."

They were early enough to avoid a long line. Ramon, Maria, and Trent were waiting at the entryway for the rest of the group. Billy, already on board, saw the gang on the dock beside the boarding ramp. "I'll come down."

Billy shuffled down the steps from the second deck on the boat to the main deck, then down to the ramp. He approached the lady taking the tickets at the stand beside the ramp. "These are the people I mentioned to you—my guests."

"Yes, sir." She motioned to the group to come aboard. "Welcome. Have a great ride."

"Thank you. Hello, Billy," Elaine greeted.

"Hello, everyone. Come with me. I will show you around. I'll be playing on the top deck, and there will be a small space for anyone who feels like dancing. But if the boat is full, they may just be standing or sitting in that space."

Like a slow-moving train, the entire group followed Billy up the steps, past two other decks, to the top deck.

Adriana panted, "My, we are up high. Look down at the dock."

Mary looked Adriana in the eyes. "Are you doing okay? Need to sit?"

"Oh no, no, I'm fine. I think."

Ramon reassured her, "Adriana, we can go to another deck if you like. The ones below have built-in benches, and it may feel more secure for you."

Maria looked a tiny bit squeamish. "I think I would like to go down a bit."

Adriana nodded and accompanied Maria and Ramon.

Elaine, Mary, and Bonnie sat with Billy and chatted. The sun began to sink, and all the lights on the boat were switched on. A small Christmas tree sat on the top deck decorated with multiple strings of lights from top to bottom. Strings of multicolored lights were stretched from the main mast to all points along the different decks, making the entire boat light up with Christmas colors. The back of the top deck had a large, blow-up Santa with lights.

"My goodness, Billy, how nice is this! So colorful."

"I never realized how many lights were on the boats in the parade," Mary noted.

"I had no idea about boat parades at all! This is the first time I have been in a boat parade and never before watched one. Look, my microphone is over there on the chair of the very small stage. I can stand or sit while I play and sing. I will probably stand as much as possible, since they are not anticipating any choppy water."

"That is good to know. I am afraid Adriana would be a total mess if we had any choppy water or wind."

"We have a great night for a smooth ride," Billy said.

"Good evening, everyone!" A loud voice boomed across the entire boat. "We have a magnificent night ahead for our boat ride. Captain Chris says everything is ready for us to depart the dock. We will pull up the plank, untie our boat, and head out in five minutes. Please move to a good spot for the tour. We don't anticipate a rough ride or rough weather. But Coast Guard Regulations require me to tell you where the life vests are. Check around; you will see several boxes or trunk-looking seats all along each level of the boat. Just lift up the lid, and you will find plenty of vests. No need to worry. We will have a smooth ride tonight."

Applause was heard around the boat.

"We are very fortunate this evening to have our local country singer on board. Give it up for Billy Wrangle!"

Applause now roared across the boat.

Billy stood, approached his mike, and said, "Thank you all. Looking forward to our little trip around the bay. Just want to say my songwriter Elaine Smith, who never takes any credit or wants to be noticed, is on board with me; and she and I have a couple of new numbers I will sing for you later on our journey. We just wrote these this week, and, well, you good folks will be the first to hear them a little later in the show."

The boat, with the engine emitting a low rumbling sound, slowly moved away from the dock.

Billy continued, "Looks like we are underway." Billy checked the tuning on his guitar and turned up the speakers. He began playing his well-known tunes first. People on the boat clapped and sang along with Billy.

"Elaine, they know all your words, all the lyrics to every song," Bonnie said.

Elaine smiled, knowing her words sent Christian messages with each line.

Elaine, Mary, and Bonnie watched all the boats get into place, forming a line that was just off the shore of the island. The water in the lagoon reflected every single red, green, white, blue, and gold Christmas light on each boat.

As they departed, Bonnie gestured. "Look on shore. All those people get to see this fabulous parade go by, and that is wonderful. But being a part of it is more fun than I knew!"

Mary agreed. "Bonnie, you had a terrific idea! Thanks for putting it out there."

"You're welcome. We were lucky Billy arranged for us to come onboard with him."

"It was a wonderful blessing, indeed," Elaine agreed.

Billy played his tunes for about forty-five minutes as the boat meandered along the shore. He took a short break. When he returned, he announced, "Ladies and gentlemen, the next two songs are our newest ones. Now, these will be part of a Christmas album that will be released next Christmas. So, you all are the first to hear them."

Billy played the first song about Christmas night and the amazing birth of Jesus. It was Elaine's favorite of the two because she liked the melody. Billy was tweaking the melody of the second song, and she knew it would be just as beautiful once he finished it. She knew they had several more songs to write before the album could be recorded. But they had a good start.

The second song was about Christmas and the total acceptance of the Baby in the hearts of mankind. Once again, she felt she was being nudged. She knew she wanted to find Chris and see if God would put the words in her mouth she needed to say. She believed He would. She trusted Him.

At the end of the second new song, the crowd once again exploded with applause. Elaine stood up. "Bonnie, I'm going to see if I can find Chris."

"Want me to come along?"

"No need. Stay with Mary up here and listen to Billy sing."

Bonnie nodded.

Anxiety filled the pit of Elaine's stomach. Would she know what to say if she got a chance to talk to Chris? She said a quick silent prayer and walked to the stairway.

# Chapter Thirteen

Elaine made her way down from the top deck to the second deck. She walked end to end. No sign of Chris. She went down to the next level. She saw what looked to be a small area blocked off a bit from the party-going crowd. Within that area, she saw lit-up screens and dials and the back of whom she assumed to be Chris. She made a beeline to his station.

She observed him for a bit, working. He seemed busy but not rushed. She waited, not wanting to disturb him. *Was this the right time?* she wondered. She said a silent prayer and asked for God's help. If He wanted her to approach Chris, she prayed for a sign. And then, she saw it. Chris took a small bottle out from under the control panel and took a sip.

*Oh no. I guess that is my cue. Help me, please,* she prayed.

"Hi, Chris."

He turned quickly, eyes glazed and a look of being found out. "Elaine. Hi."

"Just wanted to see what it is like down here, driving one of these big boats."

"Want to give it a whirl? We are allowed to let passengers drive for a few minutes in still water."

"Really? I have no clue how to do this. And it looks like we are coming upon the causeway."

"I will tell you what to do and where to steer it. It moves very slowly, so you will not do anything wrong."

"Really?"

"Here. Place your hands here and here."

Following Chris's lead, she steered the boat. "My, I never thought I would be doing this."

"I'm glad you showed up when you did."

"You are?"

"I think I might need a little help steering her in. All of a sudden, I'm feeling a little . . . fuzzy."

Elaine noticed a little of his speech was slurred. "I will do whatever you tell me to do. I trust your judgment."

"You do? My judgment?"

"Does that surprise you?"

Chris was silent and sat down in a seat beside Elaine. He looked down, sad, lonely, desolate, lost.

Elaine allowed the silence. She let him sit for a few minutes. She felt she was supposed to give him some space. *Is now the time?* she thought. *Show me what to do, Lord.* After several minutes, she put her hand on Chris's, and he looked up at her.

"Chris, pardon me for being so bold. I just want to let you know something. You are loved. You are still His. God did not leave you."

Chris remained quiet and in thought. After some time, he said, "But, Elaine, something has bothered me for a while. You know my wife died."

"Yes. I heard that."

He was silent once again.

Elaine continued steering the boat and waiting for him to say more.

"It's just . . . I was raised in church. I knew everything about what we are supposed to do when we are married. Till death . . . right? Well, I wasn't at her side when she died. I left her. I was tired. She had been there so long—weeks. No change. The hospice nurse said I should go home and get some rest. I was exhausted. I left her . . . there . . . by herself. I feel like I disappointed her. I think I did not do what God expected of me. I have not handled her death very well." Chris looked down.

Elaine couldn't tell at first, but she thought he might be holding back tears.

"Chris, you were with her during her entire illness? Through all of her time in the hospital?"

"Yes."

"I believe she may have been waiting for you to leave. She didn't want you to see her at the very end. Sometimes, that is what happens with loved ones who are very close. They wait to transition to Heaven to keep others from having to witness it. God is kind like that. He understands when the time is right. It is His timeline, not yours. If it has been a difficult struggle, a loved one may want you to see them only at peace." Elaine did not know why she had said those words to him. The words were not her own. "She is happy now, Chris. She would want you to know she doesn't feel any pain, and she will see you again."

Chris looked up at her again, and a tear rolled down his cheek. He wiped it away quickly.

"Chris, there is nothing to forgive. It was God's timing. You did nothing wrong. God loves you."

Chris stood up. He hesitated and then hugged Elaine. "Really? She might not have wanted me to suffer by watching? She loved me that much?"

"I have heard of it happening to others."

Several silent minutes passed.

"Thank you, Elaine. You are the first person to talk to me about this. Other people just say they are sorry for me or remind me she is better off. Those words are nice but not always comforting. I think I needed to hear something else."

Chris took over the boat once again and continued the journey. As the tour neared the end, Chris said, "Elaine, I feel like . . . it seems like a weight was lifted tonight."

"I'm happy for you, Chris. I have been praying for you."

"Me? You have been praying for me?"

"Yes. You seemed like you needed God's help, His guidance to get you through this."

Chris tossed the half-full bottle in a trash container. "I don't know how to thank you. I felt so guilty for a long time, like I should have been there."

"People go to Heaven on God's time. It is always on God's time. He knew it was time for her to depart. Only He knows. You will be sad for a while. How long were you married?"

"Fifteen years. We were very close. We couldn't have children, and we wanted to adopt. That is what we were talking about when she became sick."

"You will grieve for a while. No need to rush it. My husband passed away more than twenty years ago. I still have some sad moments. But I have many more happy, loving memories of our time together. You will get there."

"You want to take back over the boat?"

Elaine smiled. "Sure. This is a great learning experience for me."

Elaine steered the boat exactly as Chris instructed. One of the staff members came by. "Chris, you and your guest need anything? Drinks? Snacks?"

"I'd like some coffee. You, Elaine?"

"Coffee would be wonderful. Thank you."

The remainder of the boat parade was filled with chatting about lighter topics. After the boat was navigated safely back to the dock, Chris said, "Thanks, Elaine, for helping me out tonight with everything."

"You are very welcome! My pleasure! And hey, I learned how to steer this big boat."

"You did and are quite good at it. Can I do anything to thank you, Elaine?"

"You could come to our parties. Bonnie and I have one on the shore, and Mary and Adriana have a party in town."

"I would like that. It would be good to be around other people, I think."

Elaine and the group reunited as they left the boat.

"That was an amazing time!" Adriana gushed. "I just never knew it would be so much fun. I wasn't even nervous!"

"It was fun," Billy agreed. "And hey, Elaine, the crowd loved the new songs. I am pumped to work on the Christmas album next week."

Elaine smiled. "Hearing the response to the new songs was terrific! A test for us."

"And I believe we passed the test with flying colors."

"I, for one, loved the new songs, just loved them," Adriana said, batting her eyes at Billy.

Bonnie looked at Elaine, "And what happened to you? After the second song finished, you disappeared."

"I was with Chris. He taught me how to drive the boat!"

"No!" Adriana gasped.

"Yes! He even told me how to navigate the causeway."

"No!" Adriana repeated.

"What?" Mary asked.

"Yes. He helped me steer right between the columns of the bridge!"

"You're kidding! It went so smoothly. Are you sure you were driving then?" Bonnie asked.

A voice from behind said, "Yes, she was." It was Chris. "She learned very quickly."

The group turned to him.

Adriana walked back to Chris. "Now, tell the truth, Chris. How much did you help her?"

"Not much. Once she learned how the boat maneuvered, she was on her own."

Mary and Bonnie both clapped.

"Bravo!" Adriana said.

Elaine smiled. She knew in her heart the most important thing that had happened at the captain's station wasn't her learning how to steer a boat. The most amazing thing that had happened was her talk with Chris. She wasn't sure how much of a difference her conversation had; but one thing she did know, Chris appeared to hear her. She felt she had done what God asked her to do: plant the seed. *Let Him do the watering*, she thought.

Elaine turned and said, "Goodnight, Chris. Thanks for the lesson."

Chris nodded. "You're welcome." He watched as the ladies said their goodbyes.

"Goodnight, ladies," Mary yelled. "I'm going to drop Adriana off at her house. See you all at the Church on the Shore. Don't be late!"

Adriana waved her jangling bracelets. "Night, girls."

Ramon, Trent, and Maria walked with Bonnie and Elaine to the car. They said their goodbyes and took off for Sabal Palms.

Within thirty minutes, Elaine was back at her cottage. It had been a very long day full of excitement and new adventures.

She opened her cottage door and was greeted by a wiggly dog, who was elated Elaine was home at last. "Hello, Miss Bella. Let's go out back for a few minutes."

Once Bella had visited the backyard and returned to the deck, Elaine turned off her porchlight and locked up the cottage. She wanted to write. She felt she had enough energy to write a few pages of her children's Christmas book.

She turned on the light at her desk and began. She had decided what the story would be. She would write a book about ornaments—talking ornaments—who would learn the true meaning of Christmas. The plot was completely in her mind, and she played around with some titles. Perhaps the word *ornaments* should be in the title. But it would not be about any typical, everyday Christmas ornaments. She would write about the misfit, lonely, partially scratched-up ornaments. Maybe the title should have the word *misfits* . . . no, wait—*oddballs*.

After all, the story would be about the oddball ornaments within the collection of regular ornaments.

She smiled and turned off the typewriter and the desk lamp.

*"Oddball Ornaments."* She laughed. *I guess we are all a little bit like that.*

Her mind wandered back to Chris—the look in his eyes, the tears, the relief. She would pray for him. She would make attempts to include him, mentor him, help him to grieve however God directed.

"Bella let's go to bed. Must walk early tomorrow and make it to church on time."

Bella ran to her bed and settled in.

# Chapter Fourteen

Elaine's phone sounded her alarm. She was afraid she might oversleep and had set the phone alarm for fear she would miss church. It was a good thing, too. She stretched and put her toes into her bedside flip flops.

"Bella, you didn't wake up either," she said.

Bella stretched and looked at Elaine. Even Bella looked sleepy.

"Okay, come on. I'll let you out and get ready for a quick walk before breakfast."

Watching Bella go to the backyard, Elaine's mind suddenly flashed back to the unusually wonderful day she'd had yesterday: decorating the church tree, along with the entire sanctuary; the ladies' council providing an outstanding lunch; the new adventure of the season, the boat parade with the entire group; hearing the new Christmas songs being played by Billy for the first time. But the highlight of her day—in fact, the highlight of the past few years—was that she was able to talk to Chris, a seemingly lost soul, about God and the passing of his wife.

She thought about the words she had told Chris and knew she was able to talk to him because God gave her the courage and the right words to say. It wasn't as difficult as she had imagined it might be. She said a prayer thanking God for His help.

Bella ran back up the stairs.

"Okay, girl. I'll put on my walking pants and shoes and be ready in a flash. Here, let me get your breakfast. You can eat while I change."

There were a few words Bella understood quiet well. *Bed, eat, breakfast,* and *walk* she understood and acted upon. Elaine believed Bella was the best rescue dog ever.

Bella ate, then waited on Elaine.

"I'm ready. Let's go see if Bonnie is on her porch."

Elaine and Bella reached Bonnie's cottage and, as expected, Bonnie was waiting.

"Hey, Elaine. Short walk today?"

"Yes."

"Good. It will be fun to observe the congregation when they see the decorations."

"I agree. If we see Cara and Juan this morning at church, we should give them the heads-up about our upcoming parties."

"Yes. We added them on the list last year," Bonnie said.

Elaine, Bonnie, and Bella walked along the shore to about half the distance of their usual walks.

Bonnie turned to Elaine. "We should head back home."

"Okay. Look at the white pelicans over there," Elaine said.

"It is that time of year. I'm sure Mary will be having a field day watching the birds flying in today."

"She does love her shorebirds." Elaine laughed.

"And turtles, and ocelots, and bobcats, and jaguarundis, and, uh . . ."

Elaine laughed again. "Don't forget the whales, manatees—well, just about everything."

"Except maybe alligators." Bonnie snickered.

"And mosquitoes!" Elaine chuckled.

Bonnie and Elaine stopped in front of Bonnie's cottage while Bella chased a seagull on the edge of the water.

Elaine looked at her watch. "Oh, goodness. I'd better get back and get ready for church. I haven't eaten yet."

Bonnie started up her stairway. "Me either. But just planning on sugar-free cereal and almond milk."

"Good idea. Think I need more coffee, too."

The walk ended after only twenty minutes. Bonnie walked back up her steps.

Elaine yelled, "See you in a bit."

"Thanks, Elaine. Say, want to stop by after church for lunch? I have a few things ready to throw together."

"Sure. Sounds good."

"I'll ask Mary and Adriana at church."

Elaine and Bonnie closed the car doors and walked to the front door of the church.

"Listen to that sweet music," Elaine said.

"Heavens to Betsy, the new sound system Pastor Sam put in makes a difference. Can hear the music clear to the parking lot," Bonnie noted.

"It's beautiful. I love Christmas hymns."

A small crowd gathered on the porch of the church and slowly made their way through the doorway. Pastor Sam stood at the door and greeted each person, shaking their hand, and telling each one, "Merry Christmas."

The crowd moved into the sanctuary at a slow pace and quietly murmured words of appreciation as they scanned the newly decorated house of worship.

Pastor Sam smiled and extended his hand to Elaine and Bonnie as they entered. "Good morning, ladies. The sanctuary looks very special indeed. You did another outstanding job. Merry Christmas."

Elaine and Bonnie took their usual places near the front of the church. On the row behind them sat Maria, Ramon, and Trent; and today, Billy joined the group. Mary entered next and sat on the row with Elaine and Bonnie.

As predictable as the sunrise or sunset, Adriana waltzed in last of the group, wearing a light-weight, white winter sweater dotted with beads and pearls; white pants; a long, silver chain around her neck; and white pumps. The fragrance of the evergreen tree was no match for Adriana's perfume, which engulfed the sanctuary as soon as Adriana was greeted at the doorway by Pastor Sam.

"She's here," Bonnie said. "At least, her perfume is here."

Mary giggled.

As the last of the congregation took their seats, the small group of instrumentalists played "Joy to the World."

At the end of the song, from out of nowhere, bells were heard ringing, tinkling, and chiming a new song.

Elaine turned to discover the origin of the magnificent sounds. From the back of the church, the handbell choir entered wearing long, white robes and white gloves and perfectly playing bells made of shiny bronze.

"Oh, that is one of my favorites," Elaine said. "'Carol of the Bells.'"

The handbell choir walked slowly to the front of the church, with Pastor Sam following behind the processional. Once near the altar, the choir split into two lines, each one walking upon the small stage at the front and taking a designated position.

The handbell choir completed their first song, and then began to play "O Come, O Come, Emmanuel." During the second verse, the rest of the instruments joined in, and the music completely filled the sanctuary.

Elaine looked around at the beautifully decorated church, complete with garlands and ribbons; the beautiful, towering tree; and the candles flickering by the altar. Her eyes teared up as she was overcome with the spirit of the Savior's birth. The choir sang out, "Rejoice! Rejoice! Emmanuel . . . "

At that very moment, Elaine felt a hand touch her hand. She turned to find Chris standing beside her. Her tears flowed.

"Merry Christmas, Elaine," he said as he hugged her.

"You came," she said quietly.

"Yes. I am here." He smiled and hugged her again.

Bonnie and Mary nodded at Chris and smiled. Ramon, Trent, and Billy patted Chris on the back, and Maria gave him a big smile and a nod.

Now, Elaine was certain. This *was* the best Christmas she'd had in many years. There were two more weeks of the Christmas season to go before Christmas Day, and Elaine was full of not only the Christmas spirit but also God's love for all mankind. She knew she was blessed to be here, in Sabal Palms, with her friends, and to witness another Christian coming back to God.

Pastor Sam's sermon was perfect for the day. It was full of messages about the true meaning of Christmas and the reason God sent His Son. The pastor included examples of forgiveness and unconditional love.

Elaine glanced at Chris. He listened intently to every word. When the next hymns were sung, he opened his hymnal and sang right along. He went to the altar and participated in Communion.

At the conclusion of the sermon, as usual, Pastor Sam invited anyone who needed prayer, or to speak to him about accepting Christ, or any other aspect of worship to join him at the altar after the service. Chris waited until the last song was completed and the benediction was given. As the congregation began to leave, Chris joined Pastor Sam at the front of the church and spoke with him.

Elaine waited.

Bonnie nudged Elaine. "Want to ask him over for lunch? In fact, let's ask the whole gang."

"Yes. I'll ask him."

Bonnie turned toward the door and said, "I'll catch the others and ask."

Chris returned to Elaine at the pew. "He is a nice fellow."

"Yes, Pastor Sam is a wonderful pastor."

"Told him I wanted to become a member. He asked me to come by next week and visit."

"That is wonderful news. I believe you will enjoy coming here on Sundays."

"I feel pretty good, Elaine. Like you said, it will take time. But I know in my heart that God accepts me and loves me. I know my wife is in Heaven and no longer in pain. Well, I don't know. Somehow, I just feel a little better today. Not great, but I will get better."

"So glad to hear that, Chris. Say, how about joining us for lunch at Bonnie's cottage?"

"On the shore?"

"Yes. She and I both live nearby."

"You sure it's okay?"

"I am. It was Bonnie's idea."

"Really? So nice of her."

"Chris, we all support each other here. We have been friends for more than twenty years. You are welcome to come see us any time at all."

"Thank you."

"Want to follow me over to Bonnie's house?"

"Thanks. I will. I'm in the red truck near the end of the parking lot."

Bonnie met Elaine and Chris as they exited the church.

"Everyone coming?" Elaine asked.

"Yes. Maria and Ramon are going by their house to pick up some fresh veggies and homemade tortillas. And, Chris, Ramon asked me to tell you the lot will not open this afternoon. He will open first thing in the morning. He said there are only a handful of trees left."

"Okay, thanks. An extra day off. I will follow you, Elaine."

And that was how the Christmas season at Sabal Palms began.

Next in the *Sabal Palms* series . . .

# Sabal Palms and the
# Stormy Past

For more information about
# Terry Overton
and
*Christmas at Sabal Palms*
please visit:

www.terryovertonbooks.com
www.facebook.com/allthingspossiblewithhim
@terryoverton6

Ambassador International's mission is to magnify the Lord Jesus Christ
and promote His Gospel through the written word.

We believe through the publication of Christian literature, Jesus Christ and
His Word will be exalted, believers will be strengthened in their walk with
Him, and the lost will be directed to Jesus Christ as the only way of salvation.

For more information about
AMBASSADOR INTERNATIONAL
please visit:

*www.ambassador-international.com*
*@AmbassadorIntl*
*www.facebook.com/AmbassadorIntl*

*Thank you for reading this book. Please consider leaving us a
review on your social media, favorite retailer's website,
Goodreads or Bookbub, or our website.*

## More from Ambassador International

Sarah Bakker has spent years getting over her love for Michael Thomas. After he went MIA, Sarah thought her heart would never heal. But when he is found alive and returns home, Sarah is thrown together with him to prepare for the town's annual Christmas pageant. Perhaps Sarah will finally find the love she longs for—even if it's only in her dreams.

After Catherine Reed's husband dies, she moves back home in order to accept a new position as the teacher for the town's one-room schoolhouse. Samuel Harris has suffered his own loss and guilt has burdened him ever since. When his old flame comes back to town, he wonders if they can find healing together . . .

Sam Anthem has always been a team player, leading his Home Team on secret missions around the world. When he is forced on a vacation, he is introduced to a former covert ops soldier-turned pastor. But the vacation takes a turn when the Home Team comes under attack. As the team fights to stay alive against an unknown adversary, Sam begins to wonder if there is more to life than just the job. With his life on the line, Sam must decide between the job or his newfound faith and possible love.